Praise for the Rare Book Mystery Series

"[Thomas Shawver] weaves a tale beautifully, with wonderful, rich scenes."

— Debb's Reads

"Thomas Shawver spins an awfully good tale, full of believable characters in heightened situations, and manages to give us mysteries that are edgier than true cozies, and cozier than true hard-boileds, and feel slightly old-fashioned while still being completely contemporary."

— Biblioteca

"…What I experienced in reading this book leads me to hope that Thomas Shawver, with his own characters, his own experiences, and his own knowledge of books, will pick up Dunning's baton and lead the way to reading nirvana."

— Kittling: Books

WIDOW'S SON

Rare Book Mystery
Book 3

THOMAS SHAWVER

ROUGH
EDGES
PRESS

Widow's Son
Paperback Edition
Copyright © 2023 (As Revised) Thomas Shawver

Rough Edges Press
An Imprint of Wolfpack Publishing
9850 S. Maryland Parkway, Suite A-5 #323
Las Vegas, Nevada 89183

roughedgespress.com

Paperback ISBN 978-1-68549-288-5
eBook ISBN 978-1-68549-287-8

For the Sunday dinner gang.

"May there be a generation of children on the children of your children."

—An Irish blessing

"There are sins that can be atoned for by an offering upon an altar, as in ancient days; and there are sins that the blood of a lamb, or a calf, or of turtle dove, cannot remit, but they must be atoned for by the blood of the man."

—Brigham Young, the second Mormon prophet

"No matter what one doubts, one never doubts the faeries, for… 'they stand to reason.'"

—William Butler Yeats

WIDOW'S SON

Prologue

June 27, 1844

Four Mormons resided on the second floor of the Carthage jail when the attack began.

The mob crashed the door down, and Hyrum Smith was the first to die, felled by five musket balls. Joseph fired six shots at his brother's killer, nearly severing the man's arm. More bullets and balls poured into the room from the hallway, missing Willard Richards but wounding John Taylor. Joseph rushed to the window, only to be greeted by a seething multitude of vengeful men below.

In full-throated despair, the Mormon prophet cried out the Masonic symbol of distress, "Oh, Lord, my God, is there no help for the widow's son?"

Then bullets fired from the doorway struck him in the back so that he fell from the window. He landed on his shoulder and rolled over, unconscious. One of the militia ran forward and pulled him against a well curb. Joseph Smith opened his eyes, but there was no light in them. Colonel Levi Williams of the Warsaw militia ordered his men to "shoot the damned rascal." Four men did their duty: The Prophet was dead.

When one of the killers stepped forward to cut off Smith's head with a bowie knife, the sun shone through the overcast sky for the first time that day, illuminating the yard. The butcher's hand froze, the four who had fired the killing shots dropped their muskets, and the fear of an angry God scattered the rest.

Two nights later, a select group of Saints met in the cellar of the temple to take a sacred oath. They called themselves Danites, the shock troops of the Nauvoo Legion. Sidney Rigdon, Porter Rockwell, Lewis Dana, Bill Hickman, and Alonzo Stagg formed the sharp edge of a very bloody sword.

Each had killed without fear of earthly or heavenly retribution those apostates who had fled from Mormonism and any gentiles who dared challenge them. Each had served as personal bodyguard to the Prophet. They had been bloodied in the Missouri wars and they would be bloodied again.

In the flickering light of forty candles, they donned their special garments and sang a hymn of vengeance.

When it ended, Sidney Rigdon, self-proclaimed protector of the church, held out a bucket containing slips of paper with the names of the traitors and said, "Here you go, boys. Take these men that you can't do anything with but cut their throats and bury them. You'll be saving a wicked man's soul by spilling his blood on the ground like Joshua of old."

Lewis Dana picked the first slip. He nodded grimly when he read the name of his friend, Jonathan Dunham. The fate of Frank Worrell, a jail guard who had let the mob pass through the front door, belonged to Porter Rockwell. Bill Hickman selected Governor Thomas Ford, leaving Colonel Williams to be handled by Alonzo Stagg. But the latter insisted on trading with Hickman for the governor.

As the men prepared to leave the cellar, Alonzo Stagg proclaimed, "Because it was I who was used by the villain to take our beloved lamb to slaughter, I will avenge the blood of the Prophet in my lifetime; and I will teach my children to avenge the blood through the taking of the murderer's children and then have them teach their children and children's children to the sixth generation as long as there is one descendant of the murderers upon the earth."

Sidney Rigdon clasped Alonzo in his arms, and through manly tears, declared, "Thy will be done!" Taking from the table his own *Book of Mormon*, the one given him by Joseph Smith many years earlier, he inscribed something on the front page and dated it. Then he silently handed it to Stagg, who accepted the gift with the solemnity of a vigilant soldier.

Nearly two centuries later, three young men stood trembling before five caskets that held the bones of their ancestors. A sixth lay empty, awaiting the final avenger.

Chapter 1

One Hundred Eighty Years Later

Exit 214 onto I-80. Twelve years in that eight-by-fourteen cell behind me. Never want to see them red bluffs again. Bus ain't bad now that I got that monkey mouth behind me to shut up. Thirteen hours to KC countin' piss and eat stops. Good barbeque, I hear. What else? Hell if I know. Gotta be better than Rawlins. Best get some sleep.

"WHO WAS THE DECEASED?" the investigator from the coroner's office asked as the fire department EMTs packed up their respirator. "And why is he dressed in that getup?"

Rolls of flab stuck out between the corpse's deer-skin shirt and breeches. The long scarlet wig had slipped off the bald pate; a cheap replica of a torque hung just under the double chin. On a nearby chair, someone had set a pair of leather dancing pumps and a plastic shield. A long spear, its rubber tip bent at a forty-five-degree angle, leaned against the makeshift stage.

Neither I nor anyone in the small crowd of mostly mothers and their preteen daughters responded to the question. They were still recovering from the shock of witnessing a fifty-year-old man, who, half an hour earlier, had—with left leg extended horizontally before him, right foot tucked neatly under his bum, and back straight as the letter L—elevated twenty inches above the deck before crashing to earth in a lifeless heap.

The kids had thought it was part of the act and laughed. Now they whimpered in the arms of their horrified parents. Each of the girls but one was dressed in a sequined dance costume costing upward of a thousand dollars. The outfits had nothing Irish about them except for elaborately embroidered Celtic designs.

The fashion exception was an adolescent girl. She wore soft-toed shoes like the other dancers, but the plaid skirt and light-blue blouse were her Catholic school uniform. Perfectly straight hair, pale as an August moon, hung below her shoulders. Colorless, too, was her skin, so much so that I might have mistaken her for an albino had it not been for the orange-brown eyes that gazed straight ahead as if in a trance. She clutched a small comb in her right hand.

"This is no time for shyness," urged the investigator, whose name was Buford Higgins. "Who's the unfortunate fella?"

Natalie Phelan, she of the fiery gait and flashing temper who ran the Kansas City Celtic Heritage Center, piped up with equal bits sorrow and wonder as if the body belonged to the Savior himself. "That's Liam O'Halloran, Mr. Higgins. How could you not know?"

"Eh? Not the O'Halloran of Bog Swirl fame?"

"The very same. A few years past his prime, of course."

"More like an eternity."

Pushing aside the EMTs who had rolled a stretcher next to the stage, Higgins kneeled beside the corpse to better study the face.

When he spoke again, his voice was reverent.

"So it is, Mrs. Phelan. Sure, and he's a long way from Carnegie Hall."

During O'Halloran's salad days, he and the supporting cast of Bog Swirl had indeed performed the Cattle Raid of Cooley in that prestigious New York City venue. The Raid was O'Halloran's signature epic, played hundreds of times before thousands of enraptured fans wherever in the world the Irish Diaspora planted its tricolor flag. Millions more became acquainted through his performances on Public Television so that almost overnight, three-quarters of the English-speaking world claimed to have a touch of the green in their genes.

O'Halloran, whose real name was Augustus "Augie" Tatem of Ottumwa, Iowa, rode the wave for nearly a decade, culminating in command performances for the Taoiseach in Dublin and the Prince of Wales at Royal Albert Hall. Tens of thousands of people who wouldn't be caught dead attending a ballet had been thrilled to watch the long-haired dancer, shillelagh in one hand and pagan maiden in the other, kick, leap, and prance across an enormous stage to the sounds of thundering drums and trilling pipes.

But it couldn't last. The end of Bog Swirl came when O'Halloran broke his leg doing one too many signature backflips at a national Knights of Columbus convention in Allentown, Pennsylvania. After the last of the pipers were lured away by the siren call of a Carnival Cruise gig, O'Halloran fell to drink and dissipation.

It was Natalie's plan to bring him out of retirement in Omaha to reminisce for a few minutes about the good old days, then take a seat to watch the youngsters from the Doolan Academy perform.

Liam O'Halloran's name still carried sufficient star power to entice women of a certain age who remembered his vulpine looks and the scandalous way he winked at the audience before leaping to save sacrificial Druid virgins. And, despite their initial shock at seeing what the years and drink had done, most felt his mere presence justified the fifteen-dollar entrance fee.

Clothed in his Hound of Ulster costume, he'd talked for over an hour in a soft lilt that none of the actual immigrant Irish in the audience could quite place—Dan Regan, the Kerryman, thought it was from Connaught; the Dubliner Bannon guessed Mayo; and Mrs. Hurley, always the cynic, suggested somewhere south of Pittsburgh—but his stirring rendition of The Hunt of Sliabh Truim proved that no matter his origins, O'Halloran was a great Gael.

> *Many hundreds were in pursuit of the deer*
> *Around us on the southern hill,*
> *The battalions were on the watch for them—*
> *Fierce was the onset!*

The only boy in the Doolan Dance Academy stood

off to the side of the stage. A ginger-haired kid, he was dressed in a canary-yellow suit that made him look like a cross between Elton John and a doorman at the Hilton.

"It was Claire's fault," he said to Higgins, pointing a finger that nearly brushed the girl's cheek.

"Here now, Rory," his mother scolded. "There will be none of that."

"But it started with her, like it did with Gramma."

True or not, something strange certainly had occurred at the Center. Beautiful in one sense, horrific in hindsight. O'Halloran had finished his talk and started to climb off the low stage to polite applause when suddenly the pale girl began to sing, locking her eyes with his in a mystical embrace.

Her velvety voice was shimmering and clear and she sang in a language that might have been Gaelic, but possibly something else, something that came before that ancient tongue. Neither child nor adult moved as the mesmerizing notes wove sinuously through the room.

Then, in mid-voice, she abruptly stopped, returned to her chair, and slowly ran the comb through her hair as if nothing out of the ordinary had happened.

Long seconds passed in eerie silence until O'Halloran stepped back onto the stage.

"If you don't mind, Mrs. Phelan," he asked quietly. "Might you play a reel for me? Just one, for ol' time's sake, that I can strut to. Then we'll let the young ones show their stuff."

"I've 'Toss the Feathers' here," Natalie responded, pulling a CD from a box near the portable disc player.

"It will do fine."

Soon the room reverberated with the rhythms of

the fast fiddle. O'Halloran thrust his arms straight down on either side of his body and sprang into action, quick stepping to the 4/4 beat as if he were twenty-five again. His feet matched the ever-increasing accents on the first and third beats repeated at every eight-bar segment until he was in full glory, the great Cu Chulainn once more shedding the scales of time.

With every twirl and leap, the crowd applauded and hurrahed, oblivious to the swelling of the carotid arteries on their hero's neck. Suddenly, just as the music was to shut off, there came that final leap— accompanied, I regret to say, by a tremendous fart— and the Hound of Ulster landed on the flat of his back with feet in the air like a shot gunned pigeon.

Someone commented that for him to die of a heart attack while performing his signature backstep sweep was as fitting as it was tragic. But it was two women who had known him growing up in Ottumwa who captured him best.

"Poor Augie," Sister Mary Catherine Browne said. "He's gone to heaven, no doubt."

"Perhaps," her cousin Mary Margaret Scanlon replied. "But he won't like God."

It was only after the EMTs had wheeled the body through a side door that Higgins spotted me hovering in the back of the room holding a 1762 edition of Edmund Burke's *Account of European Settlements in America.*

I hadn't planned on seeing the performance. I was there because in a weak moment six months earlier, I'd agreed to appraise four thousand rare books that had been donated to the Center by a wealthy Irish American from Paola, Kansas, named Ted Follis.

"How's the shop doing, Mike?"

"Couldn't be better."

"That was quite a reopening you had. The place looks beautiful."

"Thanks, Major."

As soon as the word came out, I regretted it.

Buford Higgins, former lead homicide detective for the Kansas City Police Department, no longer held that position. After a thirty-year career that included the Department's highest honor, the Medal of Valor, the big man had repeatedly punched a handcuffed prisoner in front of witnesses. It didn't matter that the victim was a pedophile who had molested a five-year-old boy. The prosecutor had no choice. An hour after being charged, there came a hastily negotiated plea resulting in two years of probation, a hundred hours of community service, and thirty days of jail "shock time." The decision was still out as to whether Higgins would ever be allowed to work in law enforcement again.

The fire department would have offered Higgins temporary work, but he was too old and fat to clamber up a ladder, and by his own admission, he didn't have sufficient chemistry smarts to be a hazmat inspector. However, he asked the right questions, took good notes, and wasn't overly bothered by gore—qualities that the Jackson County Coroner's Office considered sufficient to overlook one moment's lack of judgment.

Compared to most of the grisly things Buford Higgins encountered in his line of work, the O'Halloran matter was a piece of cake.

We agreed to meet sometime for a beer when the boy named Rory appeared at our side. Looking directly at Higgins, he demanded, "Well, aren't you going to ask her?"

"Ask what, young man?"

The kid stared at Higgins as if he were dumber than a post. Then, quietly so his mother couldn't hear, he said, "Why does Claire Phelan always sing when someone is about to die?"

Chapter 2

Before opening our bookshop the next morning, Josie Majansik and I were enjoying coffee and croissants next door at Café Provence when the conversation turned to Riverrun's finances. Six months earlier we had reopened the store after being given the entire stock of high-quality books from The Book & Bell, a London antiquarian shop that had been owned by Penelope "Pillow" Wilkes. My forte being words, not ciphers, I had gratefully turned book-keeping chores over to Josie so I could concentrate on expanding our better inventory even more.

I was feeling upbeat after a buying trip the week before in New England where I'd scored literary gems by Bret Harte, Frank Norris, H. Rider Haggard, and Sarah Orne Jewett for a reasonable three thousand dollars. Before catching my flight out of Boston, I paid four hundred dollars at the Peter L. Stern Co. for Conan Doyle's *Waterloo*—a one-act play I never knew the creator of Sherlock Holmes had written—then dropped another thousand dollars at Brattle Books for a box full of eighteenth-century Americana. I was over my budget by then, but one can't be in Massachusetts and not buy something from that paragon of used-book stores.

At least that's how I'd explained it to Riverrun's Chancellor of the Exchequer when I returned to Kansas City with a suitcase full of treasures.

"So," I said, brushing the crumbs off my shirt. "How are the numbers?"

"Numbers?" Josie inquired innocently.

"Yes. As in profits."

"Oh, them," she teased. "You know how you've always promised that we'd be millionaires—or as you so elegantly put it, 'farting through silk'?"

I stared at her suspiciously. Riverrun's sales were certainly up, thanks to Pillow Wilkes's generosity, but I'd had no idea there was so much as a gleam at the end of our financial tunnel. Then again, Josie was not only beautiful, but brilliant. Who was I to question her accounting?

"At this rate," she continued while tapping her iPhone calculator, "if all goes really well, we should hit that figure by…"

She punched in a few more numbers while I waited with bated breath for the happy declaration.

"…December 2080."

"Pardon?" I smiled. "Did you mean 2025?"

"No. The third quarter of 2080," she confirmed. "Give or take a few weeks."

"But we brought in forty thousand dollars last month!"

"And spent all but two thousand of it. We're doing little better than breaking even, Michael. The debt load from the bank for the upgrades on the shop, plus your travel costs and book purchases, has tripled our expenses."

"Those trips are needed to maintain the quality of our inventory."

She bit her lip while studying the grounds in her coffee cup. I knew she was debating how direct she could be without insulting me. When she looked up again, her eyes were glistening.

"I know how hard you're working, darling. Riverrun can become as fine as any antiquarian shop in the Midwest, including Chicago. But we need to find a way to stay in business without your continually crisscrossing the country to build our stock. One solution is to entice quality dealers and their buyers to come to us. At least sometimes. That takes gaining their respect."

I nodded bitterly. "Our booth was practically ignored at the St. Louis Book Fair last month."

"It's because Riverrun isn't accredited by the ABAA. To the wealthy customers who matter, we're still just another Johnny-come-lately in flyover country peddling used books. You know what we need to do?"

"Yeah, I know." I waved to the waitress for the bill so we could go to work. "But it won't be easy."

"When has it ever been, my love?"

The Antiquarian Booksellers Association of America is as difficult to join as it is essential for success in the highly competitive world of rare books and maps. Where a dealer's reputation is everything, the ABAA's coveted logo is the stamp of that legitimacy for its members, of which there are only four hundred fifty—give or take the latest insolvency or death.

The basic requirements are that one be a rare

bookseller of good reputation (not to mention having a stellar credit rating) for four continuous years and have three current members of the ABAA willing to write letters in support.

Not long after my conversation with Josie, I called upon Charles Anthony Walsh, former Special Collections Curator for the world-famous Linda Hall Library of Science. Charlie, a friend and customer of Riverrun Books from our opening day, suggested I contact an emeritus member of the ABAA named Eulalia Darp who lived in nearby Lawrence, Kansas.

"I'm well aware of her," I said.

"Then you know that Eula's an exacting professional," the octogenarian said while handing me his reference letter typed under the embossed seal of the library. "Thirty years ago, she brokered the deal that brought the library of Sylvia Beach to the University of Kansas. Ever since then, she's been the doyenne of American bibliophiles and has never rested on her laurels. Her endorsement will sweep in the others of the Board who count. On the other hand, your chances are nil if Eula decides not to help."

"How will the selection committee even know I approached her?"

"Eula's not one to tell. But trust me, the discovery processes at the CIA and MI-6 have nothing on these folks. They'll consider her refusal a blackball."

"Say no more, Charlie. I'll just have to put the old Bevan charm in overdrive for the lady."

He peered at me over his spectacles. "On the contrary," he cautioned. "Eula distrusts flattery, even when deserved. Once you've succinctly stated your case, Michael, humility and a judicious silence are the means to gain her approval."

So it was that two days later, I drove forty miles up K-7 highway to seek the professional blessing of Eulalia Darp.

With Walsh's introduction in my pocket, I'd been reasonably optimistic that she would approve my request. But when the towers of the university drew into view on the massive hill above the Wakarusa Valley, I began to feel like an undergraduate who had failed to prepare for a final exam.

Merely labeling her "professional" didn't do justice to her renown. Eula Darp's book descriptions were legendary—never overstated or understated, always detailed, and often uncovering flaws or "points" that most dealers never knew about. It was said that she had a photographic memory, an uncanny ability to recall even the most obscure historical references to books. But that can be said of more than a few in the trade, me included.

Her major strength, one that put her at the pinnacle of bibliophiles, was her work ethic. A bloodhound in her research, she used her keen analytical mind to trace complicated provenance and unearth new treasures.

She was truly in the top echelon of the antiquarian book trade, and I suddenly felt utterly inadequate to be asking her for a favor, indeed, asking to be considered her peer.

⸻

LAWRENCE, Kansas, is a tranquil university town set at the base of the oak-forested Mount Oread where occasional student hijinks and the renowned college basketball team provide most of the excitement. But the gentle academic atmosphere belies a history so turbulent that the logo of the city is a Phoenix rising from the ashes.

It was named in honor of a wealthy Boston merchant who financed the emigration of New England abolitionists to the Kansas Territory to ensure that it entered the Union as a free state. A practical, albeit God-fearing, man, Amos A. Lawrence also wasn't above shipping Sharp rifles packed as "books" and "primers" to vigilante Jayhawkers.

Pro-slavers across the border in Missouri didn't cotton much to such things, and Bleeding Kansas became the sobriquet for pre-Civil War atrocities committed by both sides. The town was first razed to the ground in 1856, adding fuel to the already raging fury of "Osawatomie" John Brown that culminated in his raid at Harper's Ferry. Following the start of the Civil War, Missouri bushwhackers led by William Quantrill not only burned Lawrence, but killed more than a hundred and sixty defenseless men and boys. Over a century later, the last major conflagration occurred during the tumultuous anti-Vietnam War riots of 1970, when radicals placed bombs in buildings on campus and the city.

These days the old Eldridge Hotel with its fire-blackened bricks, still stands downtown on Massachusetts Street. Students, far more interested in careers than politics, proudly refer to their university (originally financed by Mr. Lawrence) as "Harvard on the Kaw River."

Eulalia Darp lived in a three-story Victorian "painted lady" halfway up the western side of the hill, where a border of Japanese maples separated it from a row of fraternities.

Dusky greens and muted chartreuse colors created a daring but tasteful charm to the outside appearance of the house. Carved wooden images of red and yellow fruits highlighted details on shutters and pillars. Every third window featured stained glass. The paint was fresh and applied with meticulous attention to detail. Beneath the steep-pitched roof were multiple dormers, detailed bracket work, and delicately carved gingerbread bordering. Stenciled squirrels, rabbits, and other critters scampered after acorns among the corbels and ribboned roofline.

A golden retriever ran alongside my Jeep when I pulled onto the long gravel driveway. Getting out, I rubbed the dog's ears and shook its proffered paw. It followed me onto the wraparound front porch, settling on its hindquarters when I rang the doorbell.

A few seconds later, I heard heavy footsteps, and a deep voice announced, "I'm comin'. Hold your horses."

The heavy oak door opened to reveal a sturdily built Native American whose head was the size, color, and shape of a bronze bowling ball, with about the same amount of hair. He wore a plain apron over a pair of jeans and faded paisley shirt with the sleeves rolled up, displaying Popeye-sized forearms.

Upon seeing him, the dog wagged its tail happily and received a biscuit in return.

"Now git back, Daisy," he ordered. "Go on back home."

Hearing our voices, a youth who had been throwing a Frisbee on the fraternity lawn next door ran up to the porch.

After securing a leash on the dog, he said, "Hey, Norm, Mom Morsley wants to see you about cleaning the chapter room at the house. We had a party last night and…"

"And a few of you young bucks got drunk and smashed up things. Don't you worry, son. Tell your housemother I'll be over shortly."

As the kid and the dog sauntered back to the fraternity, the man turned to me.

"You the book fella?"

"Guilty."

"You don' look like one."

"I suppose I don't."

"Football or hoops? I know you didn't play for the Jayhawks. I remember who all them fellas was when I coached at Haskell Indian Nations."

"I was a linebacker for Iowa. Name's Mike Bevan."

"I'm Norman Tate," he said as he extended a heavily calloused hand. "Stormin' Norman to the boys over there." He nodded in the direction of the Sigma Chi house before adding—I couldn't tell whether with nostalgia or regret—"I was their janitor for thirty years. Coaching didn't work out." He looked back at me. "A Hawkeye, you say? You know Podolak?"

"Met him once at a reunion, but he played long before me. Is Mrs. Darp in?"

"It's Miss Darp," he corrected, adding a wink. "She's a bachelor lady."

Tapping a foot impatiently, I mentioned having an appointment to see her.

"I know you do. I'm jus' wastin' time while she gets settled." He looked over his shoulder for half a minute, then back to me. "All right, you can come on in now. And let's not take too long with her, if you follow what I'm sayin'."

He led me through a high-ceilinged library stuffed

20

with leather-bound books arrayed on ten-foot shelves and heavy library tables. Half a dozen original Hudson River School landscapes in unpretentious frames completed my impression of the owner's quiet, reflective taste. A marble mantel over the fireplace boasted the works of Mark Twain, Washington Irving, Willa Cather, and Stephen Crane. The row stretched for several feet and was bound in place by Art Deco bookends featuring a pair of dancing harlequins.

Tate opened a sliding door and ushered me into a second, smaller room where three vintage kerosene oil lamps hanging from the high ceiling cast the space in an otherworldly glow. It took a few moments for my eyes to adjust to the semidarkness, but when they did, I had to check myself from doing a double take.

That's because a doppelgänger of Gertrude Stein sat with perfect posture on a chintz-covered couch before the fireplace. The couch looked as though only one person ever sat on it, and always in the same spot, exactly where she was now. On a nearby side table was a teacup and saucer with thin biscuits, the day's New York Times, a notebook and pencil, and a neat stack of files.

It was immediately apparent that the fine sense of taste that had gone into Eulalia Darp's house and collectibles did not extend to her person or attire; or maybe she preferred to focus on her possessions rather than any personal adornment.

Her hair was silver-gray, trimmed in a severely short modern style that contradicted the rest of her appearance. She wore a shapeless green jumper, undoubtedly intended to disguise her large torso, but which only made her resemble a slightly overripe pear. Large, round glasses that were in vogue in the 1950s dominated the small nose on her broad pink face. They couldn't hide, however, the intelligent brown eyes that returned my gaze with a somewhat amused expression.

Like the room, she showed wear, but her calm and self-possessed carriage reflected durability. Had she been a book, I would have described her as "tightly bound in a thick, single volume; a little worn, but in fine condition."

I wondered how she would portray me. "Stitching a little loose, slightly sprung, and outwardly cracking" perhaps?

After exchanging greetings, I'd barely settled on a wicker chair when she declared in a carefully articulated voice, "Mr. Bevan, I'm not inclined to support your application for ABAA membership. Can you provide reasons why I should?"

"Well," I began nervously. "My shop has an extensive stock of the highest quality in categories of travel, adventure, and exploration, much of it British…"

She raised a ring-bedecked hand to shush me.

"Yes, yes, I'm aware of that. But I'm mostly interested in how you acquired them."

"I fail to see how that matters, ma'am."

A faint smile. "Oh, but it does, young man. Very much so."

"They were given in exchange for services I rendered to the previous owners."

"So I've heard. The proprietors of the fabled Book & Bell of Cecil Court, London, I believe. And therein lies the rub, you see. The notoriety of Penelope Wilkes and the late Adrian Hart colors the pedigree of your cache in a most unflattering manner."

"The provenance of those books is unquestioned,"

I replied. "Wilkes and Hart had their faults, but they were devoted book people. They kept meticulous records."

She narrowed her eyes. "Faults? One is thought to have murdered a Russian client. And the other killed himself."

"Pillow, I mean, Penelope was never charged—and if she had been, it would have been ruled justifiable homicide. As for Hart's suicide, it was one of the few honorable things the man ever did."

I glanced at Norman Tate, who tapped his watch in response.

"This has been a mistake," I said, rising from the chair. "I'm sorry to have wasted your time, Miss Darp."

She looked up at me, surprised by my refusal to kowtow to her. "Please sit down. I merely wanted to give you a taste of what to expect from the Board of Governors. Some are convinced you acquired your inventory dishonestly."

She handed me a thin biscuit that had been next to the teacup.

"And please feel free to call me Eula. May I call you Michael?"

"Yes," I said, accepting the cookie and returning to the chair. "Thank you, Eula."

I paused. "Is there really so much interest in how I came to own these books? I mean, the members of the Board are wrong—I did nothing dishonest."

"There are unsettling rumors about a discovery of secret journals dating from Captain Cook's voyages," she said. "Supposedly, these journals would cast a very negative light on Cook's reputation. If true, this would send shock waves through Britain, rewriting its hallowed maritime traditions."

I remained silent, but a flickering glare through her glasses showed she expected to hear more.

"Well, what of it, Michael?"

"I'm not at liberty to say."

"Young man, every bookseller who has made something of themself has sacrificed something. It takes intellect, finances one rarely has enough of, and tremendous will. Luck is recognized, of course, but highly suspect when inexplicably abundant. The Board members are jealous of you, Michael. It isn't the question of your reputation or the provenance of your books—we booksellers are all knaves at some level. While they envy your exceptionally good fortune, I'm afraid it does not equate to respect. You must be more forthcoming on this matter to show you came by those books through good and honest effort."

My only response was to smile inwardly at the irony. I had confronted death no less than four times in New Zealand during my quest for the three journals penned by a marine on Captain Cook's historic voyages to the Pacific. It was in exchange for one of them—and the promise to never disclose the contents of the other two—that Pillow Wilkes voluntarily deeded the entire stock of her bookstore to me. I'd damned well earned them but was honor-bound to never explain why.

"I won't comment," I reiterated forcefully, making it clear I didn't appreciate being backed into a corner.

"Then you have said enough. It must be true."

"Eula, the books were a reward for something I did for Ms. Wilkes. It nearly cost me my life; it may have taken a bit of my sanity as well."

I hoped that would be enough for her, but she continued and was every bit as exacting in her questioning as she was in her catalog and book descriptions. She pressed for details, not about the explosive content of the journals, but demanding specifics about the trade-off for them. Were there loan payments? Was there a note? Is there a disclosure pending? Were you privy to their darkest secrets, perhaps? ("Blackmail is something the Board would understand," she remarked wickedly.) Had I given Ms. Wilkes something of equal value? And on and on.

I shook my head to all of it, finally gazing at a framed caricature of Marcel Proust to avoid her eyes.

When I looked back at her, there was a concerned look on her face.

"Michael, I take my role in the ABAA very seriously. Indeed, I feel somehow that my efforts over the decades have helped elevate humanity in some small way. I cannot make exceptions to my standards. Without critical evidence of your honesty and commitment to the highest degree of professionalism, I find it difficult to offer an endorsement."

She sighed, then reached over for a file, skimmed the top page, and turned back to me.

"Don't think me unfair. Your refusal to divulge a colleague's secrets is admirable. And you've been recommended by Charles Walsh, a person whom I value highly."

She sighed and placed her eyeglasses on her forehead. "Because I still wish to help you, let's try this a bit differently. Tell me about books you have acquired other than through the Book & Bell windfall?"

"My acquisitions have been rather modest, I'm afraid."

For the next twenty minutes, I relayed tales of my few significant finds in ten years of scrounging through attics and cellars for quality used books. I described my research to verify an obscure first of *A Yankee in Canada* by Henry David Thoreau and told her of my happy discovery of a complete series of Arthur Rackham illustrated at a neighbor's garage sale.

"I have firsts of Ian Fleming's later Bond novels; the full body of work of George MacDonald Fraser; and some Irish Renaissance writers such as Lady Gregory, George Russell, and—"

"Any Yeats?" she interrupted. "Joyce, perhaps?"

"Only later editions."

"I see. 'Modest' certainly was a fair description of your achievements, Michael. If you ever hope to pursue and secure the kind of books for which the rich and powerful eagerly compete—and, therefore, pay handsomely for—adequate funds and courage are not always enough. What you have so gratuitously received from Ms. Wilkes is a beginning, nothing more. You'll need more than that for the ABAA. To be a treasure hunter—and isn't that what we all are?—sometimes means becoming a pirate. It will take all the cunning, patience, and knowledge you can muster to anticipate where a rare bit of history might manifest itself."

Her dark eyes were soft now that they weren't shielded by the glasses; I felt a sense of kinship. She flipped to the second page in her file.

"I also did a little research on your background before you became a bookseller. I understand you practiced law?"

"Yes, until I was disbarred for allegedly misappropriating a client's funds."

"Oh, dear."

"A corrupt district attorney had it in for me."

I studied Proust's picture again, realizing how lame those words sounded.

"I see," she said with a little cough. "And wasn't there a more recent arrest?"

My god, she was thorough and exacting; her reputation for detailed research was only too accurate.

I looked at her directly and confessed details that she already knew.

"I was once thought to have murdered a colleague."

"Hmmm."

I noticed Norman Tate had stopped tapping his watch.

"Charges dropped," I added.

"How convenient."

"Even received a commendation."

"Fascinating. I don't recall that made it into the papers."

"No, ma'am."

"Pity."

She sighed again as she reached over to pat my hand.

"I hope you can appreciate my situation, Michael, but I have to uphold ABAA standards as well as my own. I cannot support your admission."

Bitterly disappointed but not surprised, I sat for a moment taking in the pristine copies of rare books, each carefully shielded from sunlight through their artful arrangement on the shelves. They were not just objects to Eula, but testaments to the greatness of mankind. She was doyenne of a noble profession responsible for preserving nothing less than the combined wisdom of all humanity.

Yes, Eulalia Darp had her standards. And I wasn't up to them.

"Thank you for your honesty," I said, rising to leave.

"Don't give up, Michael. Trust your instincts but aim higher. Should you happen to acquire something interesting in the near future, perhaps we might chat again."

"Something interesting" would have to be along the lines of a Shakespeare First Folio if I hoped to have a productive audience with this maven of the book trade.

As he led me to the door, Norman Tate cautioned me to never buy any ducks.

"Why not?" I asked, perplexed.

"Because with your kind of luck, they'd jus' drown."

Chapter 3

There was plenty of the morning left, but given my state of mind after the meeting in Lawrence, I'd be as useful as an ashtray on a motorcycle if I returned immediately to Riverrun.

It was a nice day and being around the campus had me feeling nostalgic. Remembering that Alice Winter had mentioned that her son, Mark, was taking summer classes at the law school, I decided to drop by Green Hall to say hello. Mark responded immediately to my text, and we agreed to meet at the student lounge in twenty minutes.

Lest you think I get a kick out of interrupting fledging barristers during their onerous studies, my reason had a real purpose. And it wasn't just to encourage him in his career path. I fancied him as a potential son-in-law.

The idea wasn't so far-fetched.

My daughter, after surviving a tumultuous experience with drugs, had spent five months at a rehab center in Lawrence. During that period, Mark, who had known Anne in high school, had been extremely supportive, even cutting law classes to check on her when she seemed particularly down. By the time Anne returned to the University of Colorado to complete her master's degree in theater studies, it seemed to Josie and me that a spark had been lit between them.

Mark's mother, however, was gob smacked when, a month earlier, I mentioned the visits.

"Mark?" she'd asked warily. "I didn't know he was seeing her."

"Yeah, almost every day," I'd responded, surprised that she wasn't aware of this. "He brought her dough-nuts, flowers, even used to play his guitar for her. I'm beginning to think there's even the possibility of a budding romance. I guess he sees some of the same things in her you do, not to mention that she's beau-tiful and adventurous. Your son's no dummy."

"Romance?" A cloud seemed to cross her face. "Please say you're joking."

"I'm not, Alice. He was wonderful to her—"

She shot a look that could have melted a bucket of diamonds.

"Listen, you," she said slowly, tonelessly. "Keep that…that…tart from my boy."

The muscles in my jaw tightened, and I made a vague sound in my throat. But before I could form words of protest, Alice had stormed off, spouting something about a "chip off the old block."

Now, it was true that my daughter's wild-ass repu-tation left something to be desired, but Mrs. Winter's virulent reaction left me more puzzled than angry. It didn't fit the gentle and dignified woman I'd known since grade school and who, until that moment, had expressed only admiration for Anne's courage in combating addiction. It was all the more shocking because Alice was normally the epitome of Junior League propriety; a gentle lady who, when not soliciting money for Haitian orphans or slinging hash with volunteers at the City Union soup kitchen, could be found organizing bingo parties at the local assisted living center.

It simply wasn't fair. Now that Anne was off drugs, she'd lost that alien, strung-out demeanor; and while she still retained the aristocratic bearing and hint of a plummy accent from her Mayfair London upbringing —all thanks to her British grandparents—the last vestiges of Sloane Ranger snobbery were gone. Equally lost, I fervently hoped, was her affinity for hell-for-leather risk taking.

Whether Alice's cosseted son was mature enough to handle the female Bevan spitfire was another thing, however.

The last time I saw Mark Winter was during his junior year in college. He'd had the easy manners of a young man rather full of himself, but not obnoxiously so. In some ways—looks particularly, but also by his knack for guileless charm—Mark reminded me of a young Cary Grant before the actor encountered Mae West.

As an adolescent, Mark had never given his parents the heebie-jeebies that Anne had supplied me with in buckets, but for the longest time, he had a lazy attitude that bugged the hell out of them. It was never my place to say anything. I figured the ever-demanding attitude of Tim Winter had a lot to do with it. Once the boy left for college, he apparently shed the mopiness, excelling in his studies while serving as president of his fraternity and lettering in baseball.

Such attributes, noble as they are, don't exactly prepare one for dating a firecracker with Vogue model looks who had nearly married Robert "Long Bob" Langston, a notorious Hollywood libertine.

I hoped to see if the young man was not only in the running for my daughter's affections but also up to the formidable task of corralling her.

Green Hall sits in a flat plain on the west side of campus. Built in the late seventies, it's a five-story glass and limestone building of nondescript architectural significance that has none of the charm of the law school's former nineteenth-century Corinthian-columned home atop Mount Oread. The newer structure's one saving grace—in my eyes at least—is that it stands next to Allen Field House, a college basketball Mecca.

The student lounge was packed with students lounging on chairs and sofas when I entered. I spotted Mark among a tense group gazing at a bulletin board with the latest test results. He was one of the few who looked genuinely pleased.

He was exactly as I'd remembered him from two years earlier; a little fuller in the face perhaps, but just as handsome. Like Michelangelo's *David*, he was broad in the shoulders and long in the flanks, with a mop of curly hair cut slightly long. His large brown eyes, dark eyebrows, and long dark lashes gave him a slightly roguish look. His upper lip was slightly narrower than the lower one, so when he smiled, which seemed to be often, you got the full dental assault.

Having seen what he wanted, Mark broke away from the cluster of students gathered around the board and made his way toward me with an outstretched hand.

"It's great to see you, Mr. Bevan."

"And you, Mark. Classes going well?"

"I'm glad to have Civil Procedure behind me, but it turned out okay. You want some coffee?"

"No, thanks. How are you doing otherwise?"

"Well, Torts…"

"I mean socially."

"Fine," he said, looking somewhat puzzled.

We both stared at our feet for a few awkward moments before I spoke again.

"Actually, I wanted to thank you."

"Sir?"

"For checking on Annie—when she was at the Allen Rehab Center. It meant a lot to her that you made the effort. For me, too."

Mark's blush said it all.

"It was my pleasure, Mr. Bevan. As a matter of fact, we remain in touch."

"Seriously? I mean, anything serious?"

His smile widened as his face grew redder. "No, nothing like that. But I'll see her in Aspen when my classes end next month. She wants me to guide her up the Maroon Bells."

I thought I knew what else that meant, but before I could say anything, he pleaded, "Don't tell my folks. Okay? Mom wouldn't approve."

My expression told him I knew it wasn't because she feared either one would topple off the mountain.

"I'm afraid that cat's out of the bag," I said. "When I mentioned to her that you guys seemed to be getting pretty close, she didn't take it very well."

He sighed heavily. "It's not like Mom to be so closed-minded about Anne. Even my dad doesn't have a problem with it."

"Your mother needs more time," I suggested unconvincingly. "At any rate, I'm delighted that you and Anne are interested in each other—as friends or whatever."

"Thanks, Mr. Bevan."

"Mike."

"Sir?"

"Call me Mike. Makes me feel younger."

I left him shortly after that, filled with joy in the knowledge that, for once, something seemed to be going right in the personal affairs of my daughter.

Silly me.

Chapter 4

I was in a much better mood after that, but before returning to the shop, I decided to take another look at the books Ted Follis had donated to the Celtic Center. Seeing all those bright, ardent students at Green Hall had rekindled fond memories of my days on Law Review at Northwestern. A leisurely hour or two sorting through the works of great Irish writers and patriots was just what I needed to restore my belief that I hadn't been a fool to give up my law career.

I also wanted to check on Natalie Phelan's state of mind after O'Halloran's tragic demise three days earlier. Even under normal circumstances, the redhead could be energetic and delightfully witty one moment, then retreat the next into a shell of silent brooding for no particular reason—a potent mixture of Maureen O'Hara and Edgar Allan Poe. I'd seen enough of my mother's struggles with manic depression to recognize that Natalie was a prime candidate for a breakdown.

Josie and I had gotten to know her when she served

as a manager next door at Café Provence. Divorced and the sole support of Claire, Natalie struggled with old student loan debts. But she was smart as a whip and the very definition of "multitasker," who never did one thing if she could accomplish four at the same time. We had helped get her the job at the Celtic Center when the president of its board mentioned to Josie that he had fired their executive director and was desperate to fill the spot.

It turned out to be a good match. Natalie, who had a degree in finance to go with her natural pluck and ability to charm the socks off the meanest Scrooge, held the line on expenses while adding cultural events to make the Center more relevant. But with Union Station's continued popularity, rents had risen, so she spent three-fourths of her time scratching for contributions. The local Irish community, a generous bunch when the plate was passed at Mass, was tight as a tick outside church doors, albeit for good reason—it's hard to press Catholic parents who are paying thousands a year for private school tuitions.

Thirty-five years old, Natalie was gorgeous. Besides having the emerald eyes of a Druid princess, high cheekbones (sprinkled with just the right amount of freckles), and shimmering auburn hair that cascaded down a swanlike neck, she possessed the kind of willowy, athletic body capable of spiking volleyballs through a hardwood floor.

It was a little before noon when I walked into the Center. A middle-aged volunteer sat at the front desk chomping on a tuna fish sandwich while reading a Maeve Binchy paperback. She looked up, licked a dab of mayonnaise from her lower lip, and nodded toward the conference room.

I thanked her and walked across a frayed carpet to a pair of opened sliding doors. Directly opposite the entrance to the boardroom was a wall featuring three rows of Irish crests that represented the family names of those who had contributed generously to the Center.

On the north and south walls were floor-to-ceiling bookshelves, with a few sets of tooled leather bindings behind the glass cases. Nice stuff, but no match for what I hoped to find in Ted Follis's cardboard banker boxes.

Natalie and her daughter sat facing each other at the end of a long oak table close to the south wall. Claire, wearing her school uniform, gazed in silence at her mother, who was giving her a quiet but heated lecture.

The pale-haired child looked pensive but not particularly concerned by the admonition. I assumed the speech was about her performance at school. Natalie had mentioned once to Josie that the principal had threatened to hold Claire back a grade for what the school psychologist had described as "behavioral idiosyncrasies."

It certainly wasn't for lack of intelligence. During weekends and school holidays, she could be found at a table in the front of our store devouring books from the history, science, and even philosophy sections. Josie had cultivated her trust by suggesting titles like David Lindberg's *The Beginnings of Western Science* and listening when the young teen seemed particularly vexed about something. But we hadn't seen her at the shop since the beginning of summer.

I've mentioned Claire's long, wispy hair, which was almost white, and the pale skin that seemed to scarcely cover the blue veins in her forearms. She was slender to the point of being anorexic, and small-boned. She was reserved as well, but none of these things made you think she was delicate.

In fact, there was an odd self-assurance about her, as if she saw things through those piercing dark-orange eyes that other people couldn't. She had some boyish features—a strong brow, jutting chin, and small hips. The same characteristics, viewed from a different angle, however, could seem very feminine, even beautiful. To that extent, there was a lot of her mother in her. But something else, too. Her father must have been an interesting-looking man.

Claire attended Ursuline Academy, a Catholic girls' school, at great financial sacrifice to Natalie. To help her mother with the costs, the fourteen-year-old worked three evenings a week at an assisted living home where she collected and washed soiled bedsheets. According to what she told Josie, she loved being among the old people, particularly when she could comfort those about to die.

The Phelans lived in a rented single-story bungalow just east of Troost Avenue, behind Rockhurst University. The neighborhood had two sides to it —one moderately poor, the other moderately well-to-do. The part nearest the college was clean, gentle, with good manners and caring families. The other was rougher—dark alleys, the rat in the road, mysterious, vaguely threatening, shabby houses sheltering wife-beaters.

It was on this unpleasant side where Claire had been raised. It was also two blocks from where I'd lived before my grandfather rescued me from my abusive dad.

I was thinking of this when the girl's head turned slowly, and she locked her x-ray eyes on mine. Natalie, having followed Claire's gaze, jumped up and rushed over to me.

"Michael, darling!" she gushed as she seized my arm. "I'm so glad you weren't scared away after the O'Halloran fiasco."

"On the contrary. I wanted to see how you were doing."

"Oh, bosh. I'm fine. Major catastrophes I can handle; it's the paper cuts that get me down."

"I know this place can provide plenty of those, but you're doing a great job. Mind if I take another peek at the Follis collection?"

"Go for it!" she urged, drawing me close enough for me to detect the scent of cinnamon in her hair. "Are the books of any real value?"

"Hard to say until I'm able to dig into the rest of the boxes. From what I've seen so far, however, it's promising."

Her nostrils flared a little, and she tightened the grip on my arm. "How promising? The Center is six months behind in rent, and the bank is threatening to call our loan if we don't start reducing the principal. Simply paying interest isn't cutting it anymore."

I furrowed my brow just enough to show my hesitancy at guessing, followed by my normally tried-and-true stall tactics.

"Yesterday, I noticed a religious tract by the Protestant Archbishop of Armagh dated 1631, and a nice work by Edmund Burke. Then there was a charming *Darby O'Gill and the Good People* that included an inscription by the author, Herminie Templeton Kavanagh. It was the McClure Company edition dated 1903, making it a true first and not the Reilly and Lee reprint…"

Natalie's eyes glazed over—a common occurrence among listeners when I start prattling about rare books or rugby union football—but when her fingernails began to draw blood from my arm, I cut to the chase and gave her what she wanted to hear. "If there is more such gold in the other boxes, I can see my appraisal going into six figures."

That stopped the glazing.

"You'll think this blasphemous, Michael, but I intend to recommend that the board sell the collection if fundraising doesn't improve."

I winced. "God, don't even think it. It's not necessary if the bank considers the books sufficient collateral."

She regarded me with a narrow smile before purring, "Then I presume your valuation will be generous."

The air got cooler as I realized my mistake in prematurely suggesting a figure. It didn't matter whether I'd mentioned hundreds of thousands of dollars or twenty-five. It was foolish and unethical to set a client's expectations without having done a complete evaluation of the stock.

I began to retract my earlier statement as to the presumed value, but Natalie wasn't listening. She had something else on her mind by now.

Releasing my arm, she turned to her daughter. "Honey, could you give Mr. Bevan and me a few minutes?"

The girl rose, performed what seemed to be a curtsy in my direction, and drifted from the boardroom.

"I'm really worried about her," Natalie confided when we were alone. "She's become so withdrawn. She only seems to enjoy being around older people. And that caterwauling! The episode before poor O'Halloran died was just one example."

"Don't you think you're being too critical? I find it refreshing that a girl her age respects the elderly. Plus, Claire certainly has a remarkable voice."

"Bullshit. It's creepy the way she hangs around the dying. Crooning them on their way to eternity! She never sang so much as a nursery rhyme until six months ago."

"Have you taken her to a doctor?"

"If you're referring to a shrink, I did. He said it's an adolescent phase she's going through."

"He's probably right, Natalie. We were all a mess at that age."

"This is different. I don't recognize my child. Despite her isolation, I don't even think she's unhappy. But something has poisoned her soul."

Natalie was prone to saying things like this—a dark power always lurking about, waiting to strike when one is happiest. It comes with red hair, I suppose.

"Has anything happened to disturb her?"

A peculiar stillness came over Natalie's face. "Possibly. I recently mentioned to her an upcoming change in our circumstances."

"What's that?"

"Emery Stagg and I are getting married."

I tried not to look shocked, but it was impossible. Lately, I had seen them dining together at Café Provence and once or twice discussing something while strolling through the bookstore, but the two were total opposites. Whereas Natalie was a lissome Celtic goddess, as good with a joke as with a song, her fiancé appeared to me to have all the charisma of a speed bump.

When he first entered Riverrun Books two years earlier, there had been nothing notable about Emery other than he looked like a pair of pliers. He was slightly less than six feet tall and lean, with sandy-brown hair too dull to be properly described as blond that was cut in what used to be called a flattop. His thin face was characterized by sharp angular features. An upturned nose deviated a half inch to the left, thin lips turned down at the corners, and closely spaced walnut-colored eyes carefully studied the world behind nondescript wire-rimmed glasses. I sensed he was physically tough but also sensitive to perceived slights. The guy had "lonely childhood" written all over him.

Everything about him seemed practical and functional. There were no adornments, no wasted words or actions, no fiddling or fussing. He dressed simply and consistently in a white button-down shirt, black trousers, skinny black belt, dark-gray socks, and brown Hush Puppy Mall Walkers. Offered a cup of coffee by Josie his first day in the bookshop, he politely declined, stating that caffeine was off-limits for a Mormon. I recall him having only two expressions at the time: a questioning gaze and purse-lipped indigestion.

All this combined to make him appear distant or disconnected, and the impression was magnified by his somber presence. I decided he was somewhere on the high end of the autism spectrum, as socially awkward as he was intellectually astute.

In those days, Natalie was waitressing part-time at Café Provence while trying to finish her business degree at Avila College. I noticed that when she was on duty, a different Emery Stagg emerged. She must have seemed completely alien to him with her gaudily painted fingernails, dangly earrings, piles of jewelry, and long, scarlet hair done up differently on any given day, but he obviously found the contrasts to be irresistible.

He would borrow a mathematics book from our shop, take it into the café, and pretend to read it until she arrived at his table to take an order. Then an amazing transformation would occur—his melancholy face would turn into one of fawning appreciation, like a puppy anticipating a biscuit from its mistress. If she left to serve other customers, his eyes followed her with a gleam that was a weird cross between adulation and guilt.

Perhaps, like me, Emery had been intrigued not so much by Natalie's adornments as by the subtle melancholy in her eyes when she wasn't bounding through the restaurant, bantering lightheartedly with her customers, creating good cheer at each table.

But I'm guessing.

What I knew for sure was that apart from the fact that they shared high IQs, Natalie was everything Emery was not—extroverted, comfortable with everyone, volcanically spirited, willing to take risks and laugh off mistakes. She had always shown him polite consideration, but I never dreamed there could be more to their relationship.

"Congratulations," I managed to mutter after Natalie found it necessary to repeat the wedding announcement. Then I hastily followed with the only compliment that came to mind, "He'll be a good provider."

Rather than thanking me, she went to close the

conference room doors, then returned to the table where I had taken a seat next to a stack of books from the Follis collection. Leaning over, she took my hands in hers.

"I know you don't think much of Emery. I suppose no one does other than those who respect his work at Becker Systems. But I adore him."

"Mind if I ask why?"

"He has poise, an air of competence, and a resolute calmness."

"That sounds fine for a curriculum vitae, but not a life partner."

Her face flushed at my bluntness.

"Because he's not vulgar nor a snob. He's not commanding or powerful or masterful. Because he's not—"

"All negatives. Do you love him or not? When you're alone with him, does he take off his face to reveal under his mask?"

"How very droll, Michael. Certainly, he's not like any man I've ever known. He's quiet, but he likes to laugh with me. He's smart but not arrogant. He's protective but not smothering. And he's open. He's willing to grow and change, causing me to improve, too. I like that. I love him because he makes me think."

She might have been describing quantum theory; this was utterly inexplicable to me as I had no idea there was anything remotely interesting in Emery. All I saw was a boring guy who didn't respond to my attempts at bonhomie. He didn't find me charming, and the feeling was mutual, so I assumed that everyone saw him as I did. How could he have such appeal to a firebrand like Natalie?

"Makes you think? What on earth do you mean by that?"

"His perspectives are different," she said with a shrug. "I can't really explain, but I find myself reliving our conversations and thinking about things in new ways. I don't know, but it feels healthy. And we have fun exploring things together."

"Things?" I tilted my head, squinted one eye, and gave her a look, pretending I conjured them making love. "How veerrry interesting."

"Oh, for Pete's sake, grow up, Mike! He's a loner, and he hasn't plugged in much to the world—movies, TV, books, music, and so on. I get to introduce him to the things I like, and he does the same for me, explaining his engineering and some of the odd things he thinks about."

She shook her head and grinned at me. "Now, mind you. He's wrong as often as any man. But he's willing to admit when he's wrong. That's not something you often see among members of your gender."

I wasn't sure how to answer that.

"Ummm, okay," I said. "I'm just surprised you'd go for a—" I almost said 'milquetoast,' "Er, fella like him. After all, he's not like your ex-husband, right?"

Whomp!

Natalie Phelan slapped me about as hard as I've ever been smacked by a woman—with the possible exception of Sister Mary Agnes Aquinas.

Have I mentioned that the redhead had a temper?

"Don't you ever mention that bastard again, Bevan!"

"What bastard?" I managed to utter while my tongue fished for loose teeth. "I never met the guy."

The emerald charcoals in her eye sockets dimmed

but continued to smolder. Her mouth spouted an apology that, when it finally came out, almost sounded sincere.

"I met Sean Phelan when I worked at a bar in Boston," she quickly added. "He was a charmer off the boat from Donegal with a quick wit and raucous laugh. But 'Take what you can, when you can' was Sean's motto. The bastard married me for a green card. In return, he gave me Claire, a broken cheekbone, and damn little else when he left us for New York."

She paused to take a breath. "And you're right, damn it. The first thing that appealed to me about Emery was that he seemed as far off the charts from Sean as I could find in a man."

The fire in her eyes dimmed. She placed a hand under my chin, lowered her face, and kissed me, lightly, on the lips.

"I'm sorry, Michael." This time it seemed genuine.

"No harm done," I said, and then risked getting smacked again. "Aside from Emery Stagg not being like your thuggish Hibernian, what else do you see in him?"

"He's not only extremely smart but also considerate. I felt sorry for him at first. His painful shyness, the halting way he spoke, was pitiful. A cloak of sadness fit him far better than his clothes. But it meant he was an introvert. Being an engineer, he tends to see everything in absolutes. Ask him if a glass is half full or half empty, and he'll say it's too large by a factor of two."

"I know the type. Either something needs to be fixed, or it will need fixing after it's been used a while."

"That's him for sure," she said with a laugh. "I'd encountered boys like him through my math classes at

Avila. I'm not one to be ignored, and it amused me to find that they barely noticed me at first. So I worked to befriend a few of the shyer ones. They sure came in handy when I needed help with calculus."

I looked at her without saying anything. She was going to have to do better than suggesting that Emery was a great math tutor to convince me why she was so smitten by the guy. And, soon enough, she did.

"Emery is different from men like you," she continued. "But I knew early on that he wasn't simply a tech dweeb. I sensed something hiding within him, a secret that he kept buried but would reexamine at times, kind of like Frodo and his ring. And that smile! It contains the whisper of a laugh that, when upon appearing, transforms him into a handsome prince. Maybe because it was so rare, I found myself figuring out ways to coax it out more often."

"Well, I, for one, have yet to see it. How'd you manage to nab the first grin?"

"Quite by accident, really. After serving him the Provence salad, with its soft-boiled egg on top of the greens and frisée, I reached across his plate to fill the water glass when his hand shot up to grab my wrist." She shivered at the memory. "I'll never forget the surprisingly electric sensation I felt at his touch. He dropped his arm as soon as it became apparent why he had done it—to prevent the outlandishly fancy lace of my cuff from being drenched in the dressing—and then he showed that elusive, enigmatic smile.

"He apologized, explaining that he didn't want me to ruin my costume. Costume! I'd spent an hour trying to decide on that outfit. But on reflection, I realized he understood me completely; more than any man—or woman, for that matter—ever had. Yes, it was a costume fit for a pirate queen. And I laughed out loud."

Natalie lapsed into silence after that, but I knew there was something else she needed to say.

"Your outburst against me a few minutes ago wasn't because I mentioned your ex, was it?"

She stood, tilted back her head, and swept back a long auburn tendril that had drooped over an eyebrow.

"Not entirely," she answered. "I've a lot on my mind these days, what with Claire, finances, preparing for the Bloomsday celebration…"

"And something else?"

She nodded.

"When Emery first came to Kansas City, Mike, it was with the sole intent to murder me."

Chapter 5

Now, if you know anything about my earlier travails, you'd understand that my first thought upon hearing that was to scurry out the side door muttering excuses about a suddenly remembered dental appointment. But I'm a sucker for a woman's tears. And Natalie Phelan, who, despite her occasional black moods, I'd never so much as seen snivel, had just become a gushing Niagara of woe.

"Jesus, when did you learn that?" I asked once my saliva ducts unjammed.

"Last week." She sobbed. "We'd just finished preparing our wedding announcement. Emery wanted no secrets between us. He said it involved something my ancestor did to Joseph Smith."

The significance of the name didn't register at first. After all, there were ten Joe Smiths in the Kansas City phone book alone. Then it struck. "The Mormon?"

"Yes," she said, dabbing her eyes. "I knew that I was a descendant of Governor Thomas Ford of Illinois, but I had no idea some Mormons held him accountable for their founder's death."

"But that was nearly two hundred years ago! What does that have to do with you now?"

"It's complicated."

"No kidding. Have you gone to the police?"

"Why would I, since it was him who admitted it? Despite my initial shock, I never felt threatened. You've met Emery. He's not capable of violence."

"Jeffrey Dahmer's mother surely felt the same about him."

She looked at me levelly, no tears now. "I trust him, Michael."

I didn't know what else to say. But Natalie did.

"Would you talk to him? He doesn't have any friends other than a few colleagues at work. Perhaps you can bring him out of his shell."

When I hesitated, she urged, "He trusts you."

"But I barely know him."

Not about to let me off the hook, Natalie Phelan appealed to what we both knew I couldn't resist. "If it helps," she said. "He also has a remarkable book he's prepared to sell. Please, Michael. Say you'll see him at your shop in the morning."

And, like an idiot, I looked into those luminous green eyes and said, "Sure, why not?"

The Emery Stagg who entered my store the next morning gripping a battered briefcase had changed slightly from two years earlier. For one thing, he'd added a little paunch at his belly, no doubt from the beer and wine I'd seen him imbibe on occasion with Natalie in the bistro. I suspect he was testing the teachings that had been drummed into him through the Church of Latter-day Saints but sought to lessen the heresy by treating his experimentation with alcohol as if it were a science project. He'd let his hair grow longer too, combing the strands straight back from his high forehead.

Lest one suspect he'd become an extrovert, however, Emery retained the look of one slightly adrift in public, like a letter delivered to the wrong address. And for all of Natalie's attempts to liberate his conservative fashion sense, he hid the tortoiseshell glasses she bought him in a sock drawer and remained steadfast to the old white shirt/black trouser uniform of the day, as if it was one less decision to make every morning. In short, Emery Stagg still looked and acted like what he was when I first met him: a civil engineer specializing in water and sewage treatment systems who felt far more comfortable among flocculation filters than people.

Approaching the counter that morning, he looked concerned to find Josie standing next to me.

"Hiya, Em," she called out cheerfully, instantly attuned to his unease. She tucked a pencil behind her ear and made a show of gathering up a bundle of papers to clear space next to the computer. "Why don't you two get comfortable in the alcove? Mind if I join you after I finish these accounts?"

He drummed his fingers on the counter, considering.

"Okay, I guess," he finally answered.

Emery followed me to a quiet section of the shop between the philosophy and poetry sections where we settled into green leather wingback chairs.

"You must think me nuts," he began softly, setting his briefcase on the coffee table between us.

I was tempted to respond sarcastically with something like, "Because you intended to murder Natalie? Or that you confessed it to her after changing your mind?"

But I didn't. The introvert was trying his best to be forthcoming about a matter obviously painful to him, and I didn't want the conversation to end before it began.

Instead, I smiled diplomatically while my left index finger explored an ear.

"One can't hide a secret as dark as that forever," he continued, looking at me with bleak, tired eyes. "She needed to know before deciding to accept me."

"Given what she told me last night," I said, "you don't have to worry on that score. She loves you very much."

Emery rubbed his nose between his thumb and forefinger, stifling a sniff.

"Becker Systems lost its contract with the county," he said, drawing a handkerchief from his back pocket. "I may lose my job. At best, my billable hours will be cut. We are going to need money. It's the only reason I agreed to see you."

So much for Natalie's claim that he sought a friend.

He pressed the brass latch to open the briefcase.

At first glance, the book seemed like nothing special. It was bound in what looked to be original brown calfskin, but it had been rebacked with a new leather spine featuring a gold-embossed title that said *Book of Mormon*. An early edition of that was not uncommon in Jackson County, Missouri, where Joseph Smith had first settled, and which remained home to thousands of Saints and a magnificent RLDS temple. True firsts, however, were another matter. Of the five thousand original copies, only a few hundred remained in circulation.

Without lifting the book from the case, I carefully opened it to the first end sheet. The page was blank except for an inscription:

Presented by Sidney Rigdon, June 28, 1844, to Alonzo Stagg, a faithful Danite who will hath Trampled the traitors into the earth.

You get to know something about Mormon history if you live in this part of the country, which Joseph Smith declared to be the site of the biblical Garden of Eden. The local population in Western Missouri had initially welcomed the industrious and clean-living people who had been forced to flee Kirtland, Ohio, in the 1830s. But the Saints' close-knit ways of buying up land and garnering blocs of votes soon upset the welcome wagon. Furthermore, their dismissive attitude toward other faiths soon turned them into enemies of the hard-heeled settlers who had wrested the land from savage Indians, cleared the forests, and tamed the prairie. Eventually, both sides committed atrocities.

Sidney Rigdon, self-proclaimed Protector of the Church, used the Danites not only to protect his people from the "gentiles" but also to force dissenters —those who didn't offer blind obedience to the teachings of the Prophet—to leave the Mormon-held counties under threat of death.

I looked up at Emery. "Was Alonzo Stagg a relative?"

He smiled wryly. "My great-great-great-grandfather."

I turned my attention to the cover page. It was

heavily toned and foxed with rust like spots on paper considered inferior for the time:

THE
BOOK OF MORMON
AN ACCOUNT WRITTEN BY THE HAND OF MORMON,
UPON PLATES TAKEN FROM
THE PLATES OF NEPHI

Beneath the two paragraphs of the prologue were the all-important words:

BY JOSEPH SMITH, JUNIOR,
AUTHOR AND PROPRIETOR.
PALMYRA:
PRINTED BY E.B. GRANDIN FOR THE
AUTHOR.
1830.

This was a true first edition, published in Palmyra, New York. I knew this because subsequent printings had eliminated the words identifying Smith as author once he'd proclaimed God's words had been dictated directly to him through the angel Moroni.

In addition to its rarity, this book was incredibly important to religion scholars because of changes Smith made to the text in later editions.

Seeing my reaction, Emery's eyes sharpened. "What can I get for it?"

I had no qualms this time suggesting a price, knowing that prices for original Mormon works had skyrocketed in the past five years. A Palmyra first edition inscribed by an early LDS apostle went for more than double the estimate at a recent Swann Galleries auction.

"Because of its historic association," I said, gently closing the book, "I figure two hundred grand. Perhaps a quarter million."

Emery leaned back, clasped his hands behind his neck, and closed his eyes. "How soon can you find a buyer?"

Thoughts of Eulalia Darp and the ABAA suddenly ricocheted inside my frontal lobe.

"That depends," I answered. "Leave the book with me. I'll call some dealers and get back to you in a couple of days."

Emery opened his eyes. They were a little wet.

"Must be tough giving up such an heirloom," I said.

"You don't know the half of it. For most of my life, that book represented my entire being. The inscription that you find so valuable is what, until I came to realize that Natalie truly loved me, bound me to a murderous legacy."

Then he proceeded to tell me why.

Chapter 6

Celtic Heritage Center? Didn't know they had that many micks in this part of the world. If they got 'em up in Butte, I suppose they're everywhere. Hear tell they breed like rabbits. Like us Mormons. So that's her? Good lookin'; I'll give her that. Tall, leggy gal. Nice tits, too. Cool the urges. Not why I'm here. Still, it seems a waste to do what's gotta be done. There'll be plenty of time afterward for the ladies.

▭

EMERY HAD a way of talking as if conversing with himself. It wasn't as if he was trying to be coy or arrogant. He simply trusted his own company more than that of others. But he had something he needed to share, and I was the most convenient conduit.

"At fourteen," he began, "I was short and fat, and I had as much gumption as a soft-shell crab. All I wanted to do was take things apart so I could put them together again. I'd been lax in my religious studies and hadn't given personal testimony in months. People in

56

my ward were beginning to say I was lacking in the spirit. One night I was swapping out the memory board on my computer when my father came into my room to tell me I was to spend that summer at his brother's ranch. He said it would put starch in my spine and more love for Jesus in my heart. It really shocked me."

"Why?"

"My parents were regular LDS Church members. They prayed to see a time when all would walk in the footsteps of the Great Exemplar, the Lord Jesus Christ. But they weren't overly fervent, realizing that the world can't be converted in a day. My uncles and aunts, however, belonged to a fundamentalist offshoot that was off the chart of accepted LDS teachings. Mom called them 'religious tumbleweeds.'

"Listening to their late-night talks when they thought I was asleep, I learned that Uncle Lamar once had three wives in addition to Aunt Regina when they lived in Canada. But there was something even more shocking than polygamy in his background."

"Don't tell me he voted for the former president," I said, hoping to stave off a stultifying lecture on religious apostasy.

"Blood atonement," Emery whispered, ignoring my feeble attempt at humor. "The doctrine that sometimes to save a person's soul you had to spill their blood."

"Like when blood brothers prick their fingers?"

He looked at me as if I weren't taking any of his stories seriously.

"No, Bevan. Like cutting someone's throat to avenge a wrong."

For a moment, I thought he was the one being

sarcastic. But his expressionless face made it clear he was incapable of irony. I suppressed a shudder.

"Why on earth would your parents send you to someone who believed in that stuff?"

"Lamar was my father's older brother, and he still held him in awe. When Lamar insisted that he no longer took the concept literally, Dad chose to believe him. After all, it was something that was considered merely allegorical even by wild offshoots like the Kingston clan. My mother wasn't so naïve. But when she challenged him, Lamar laid into her. He said she should be more concerned about my physical and spiritual development, not worrying about old-time Danite spook stories."

"So off you went to a Mormon boot camp," I said.

"Some might say that, but it wasn't regimented, at least not in the beginning. My uncle and aunt lived a few miles west of Grand Lake, Colorado, in a large pine lodge along the Tonahutu River. Dad practically had to shove me out of the car I was so terrified. I soon discovered, however, that the solitude of a beautiful mountain setting offered an attractive alternative to the kids who made fun of me at my suburban high school. Nor was Uncle Lamar the ogre I'd feared him to be. With his grizzled gray beard and bloodhound eyes, he looked like an old-time prophet. But when he wasn't pontificating about some religious thing, there was a gentle, even humorous side to him that was utterly charming. I'd never known a man like him."

"What was your aunt like?"

"Regina was a jolly, round-faced woman fifteen years Lamar's junior who covered her full figure in calico and wore braids that hung on either side of her shoulders. She was very pious but didn't seem overly traditional even though Lamar insisted she wear an old-fashioned white cap. She'd been a soloist with the Tabernacle Choir before she met Lamar. They didn't have children—a real curse for Mormons that must have weighed heavily on them—and I figured that's why they were always hosting their relatives' kids."

As Emery began to describe how twelve cousins joined him at the lodge that first summer, Josie suddenly appeared with a plate of brownies from the bistro.

"What'd I miss?" she asked, passing around the goodies.

"I'll tell you some Sunday," I said as she settled in a chair next to me. "Go on, Emery."

He took a bite first, grunted approvingly, then took another.

"I got picked on by a few of my cousins," he finally said, brushing crumbs from his shirt. "But that stopped when I made myself useful to Lamar fixing the tractor and doing other mechanical things. After that, it was hands-off me. The only exception was Porter Grint. He was scrawny back then but mean as a wounded badger. He didn't feel pain like a normal person either, always sticking himself with a knife or daring others to bet on how long he could hold a lit match under the palm of his hand.

"Regina taught us hymns along with Mormon history lessons while Lamar concentrated on showing us how to hunt and live off the land. I'd never liked the Boy Scouts, finding campouts an uncomfortable waste of time when I could be making something in the garage. But I was surprised to discover that I enjoyed the demanding outdoor training under my uncle's guidance.

"The next summer, we learned how to survive in the wild for considerably longer periods. That's when I really began to flourish. I'd grown to the height I am now, and while still no athlete, I was no longer Porter's punching bag. By the third year, the number of cousins invited back was down to five, and our outdoor orientation escalated.

"At sixteen, I underwent the endowment ceremony for the Aaronic priesthood at our temple in Ogden. Usually this occurs when a Mormon is preparing to go on a mission following high school. But, as I was to learn during another ceremony at Staggs' Lodge, it was essential that I be purified for an entirely different reason.

"After being washed and anointed, I donned white garments with a green satin apron in the shape of Adam's fig leaf. I was given a name by which I was to be known in heaven, learned a whole series of secret handshakes, words, and penalties, and then passed through the veil to enter the Holy Priesthood."

"Good for you," I said, stretching my legs. "Did you take up a collection?"

Josie kicked my ankle and Emery gamely continued.

"The next summer, only Porter Grint, Dennis Dietz, and I were invited back to our uncle's compound. This time we were completely cut off from the outside world. No more river rafting or trips into Grand Lake with Regina for supplies.

"I was glad to see Denny sitting at the breakfast table that first morning behind an enormous stack of pancakes slathered in butter and syrup. He was a surfer dude from San Diego and one of those good-natured true believers who couldn't hear enough about the wars between the Nephites and the Lamanites as chronicled by Mormon, the father of Moroni.

"I think if we'd been allowed to celebrate Halloween, Denny would have pasted on a beard and trick-or-treated as Brigham Young. Not only was he good-looking and rich—his father owned the largest Toyota dealership in Southern California—but he also had a playful sense of humor, getting Regina to giggle like a girl with his slightly off-color jokes. 'How many gentiles does it take to enter an outhouse?' That sort of thing. Denny had always been nice to me as well. I liked him a lot.

"Porter hadn't changed much, though—still mean and foulmouthed when Lamar wasn't around—and not the brightest bulb. I suppose there were reasons for the way he was. Aunt Louise preferred her dozen parakeets to people and that included her son. Porter told me she used to beat him with a cane whenever he failed to keep the birds' water and food dishes full. His father never intervened. The only time either of them showed any affection was when he came home from school with a split lip or black eye."

I muttered something about being a member of that same club. But, by now, Emery was only listening to himself.

"Porter made up for his deficiencies by being a fine shot and the first of us to master the complicated handshakes, secret words, and oath penalties. The outlawed Danite gestures pertaining to throat cutting and disemboweling were particularly appealing to him. He was descended from Orrin Porter Rockwell, Brigham Young's notorious bodyguard, and he couldn't have been prouder that he shared the name.

That final summer and into October, our training radically changed."

"I suspect there was a move from physical challenges to enhancing mental ones," I said, recalling my Marine experience."

Emery nodded. "During the next phase, Lamar maintained our physical workouts but also interspersed it with lectures on the martyrdom of Joseph Smith and his brother. The indoctrination was constant and repetitive with lots of emphasis on the atrocities committed against our ancestors during the Missouri-Mormon War of 1838.

"Others we had never seen before took over much of our training. They were hard, no-nonsense men, nonrelatives who regarded us three boys as nothing more than worms to be transformed into creatures of their own reckoning. We were told that outsiders, even those Mormons like my parents and siblings, and the cousins who had been to previous camps and found wanting, clung to the wrong beliefs and were dangerous. We were never allowed more than four hours of sleep a night. Unlike before, we wore the same unwashed dungarees and cotton shirts for days at a time. There was no free time for math equations or tinkering with machines. All decision-making was controlled by Lamar and his men. Regina had left the compound. We had no tasks other than to obey commands. We were often isolated from each other except when we had to stand and recite our wrongful thoughts and then be subjected to the criticism of our instructors. Even Porter broke down at times. His cursing stopped, as did his bullying.

"Denny took it hardest, however. He'd become dull and lackluster, a drone. It was as if his exuberant spirit had died. Only when receiving praise from our uncle, did he break out of his zombielike trance. Then the light of God shone upon him.

"Looking back on it, I suppose the same description would apply to me. Despite the hardships, for the first time in my life, I felt part of something greater than myself."

"It's hard to believe you could be so naïve," I commented. "You must have had some inkling of what the training was leading to."

Josie, who had been shaking her head and grimacing throughout Emery's monologue, came to his defense.

"The three of them were, what, only sixteen or seventeen then?" she asked. "Cut off from the rest of the world, they would have needed extraordinary mental strength and will to realize what was happening to them. It sounds like Lamar's methods were straight out of the brainwashing handbook. To be immersed in that kind of environment would give anyone a distorted sense of reality. In most cases like this, there are serious ramifications—science is still learning how the mind adapts to prolonged mistreatment." She reached for Emery's hand. "How did you adjust?"

Rather than answer, he pulled his hand away and avoided her eyes.

"Did you have nightmares?" she prompted. "Or trouble getting back into normal society when you went home?"

This time it was I who nudged her under the table. It was painfully obvious he'd always had trouble integrating into society—and it wasn't just due to any psychological torture at his uncle's camp for wayward boys.

But to my surprise, Emery flashed a smile, the first evidence I'd seen that he could be happy. I thought of Natalie's description. She was right. It was like the whisper of a laugh.

"I don't know," he finally answered. "I was never that good in a group to begin with. I'm not trying to defend myself, but we had become so controlled that we believed departing from their commands meant eternal damnation. It wasn't until our knife-handling lessons went from practicing on straw dummies to killing sheep that I finally began to suspect the purpose for which we'd been selected."

He hesitated a moment, but the smile remained as he focused on Josie. "I liked the feeling of control. I suddenly had power. It was intoxicating. At certain times I still feel it."

"I'm not sure that's something you want to advertise," she warned.

His smile dissolved. "Not to worry," he answered. "I know it was madness."

"So what happened next?" she asked.

"On our last day, we awoke to find cars with license plates from Utah, Arizona, and California parked outside the main lodge. Porter, Denny, and I were kept in our rooms without food or water. Late that night, after being told to put on our endowment garments, we were blindfolded by a masked figure in a long-hooded robe. He led us to an outbuilding that had been off-limits to us before."

Josie and I exchanged looks. I can't speak for her, but I was finding all these references to throat cutting and secret pacts by vengeful zealots damned disconcerting. For his part, Emery was really getting into it, his normally placid eyes gleaming with excitement at the recollection.

The store was filling with customers. Josie excused herself to return to the counter. Emery politely stood as she left, then sat down again to continue his tale.

"I heard the door open and felt the presence of several other men. They guided us into the building and down a stairwell to a dank basement. We stood still for an uncomfortable length of time in the chilled atmosphere, listening to the shuffling of robes gathering around us. Finally, the gravelly voice of Uncle Lamar addressed us with the words of the second Mormon prophet, Brigham Young."

Emery's voice suddenly altered as if he were having an out-of-body experience—for all I know, maybe he was. Whatever the case, I have no doubt that what I heard next were the exact words declared to him and his two cousins.

"'There are sins that men commit for which they cannot receive forgiveness in this world, or in that which is to come, and if they had their eyes open to see their true condition, they would be perfectly willing to have their blood spilled upon the ground, that the smoke thereof might ascend to heaven as an offering for their sins; and the smoking incense would atone for their sins, whereas, if such is not the case, they will stick to them and remain upon them in the spirit world. There are sins that can be atoned for by an offering upon an altar, as in ancient days; and there are sins that the blood of a lamb, or a calf, or of turtle dove, cannot remit, but they must be atoned for by the blood of man.'"

Emery reverted to his regular voice to explain. "I'd heard the blood atonement speech before, but until then, it had always been mentioned as a parable or a theoretical principle, like the gruesome penalties of the Old Testament that no one took seriously anymore. Now, however, I understood that everyone standing before us in that chamber meant to apply this chilling doctrine literally.

"We next heard three taps of a cane on the floor, followed by a different tapping in response and the ringing of a bell. A new voice commanded the three of us to join hands and recite the old Mormon oath.

"'We and each of us,'" we began, "'do covenant and promise that we will not reveal the secrets of this…'

"'Investiture,' the voice cued helpfully.

"'…investiture. Should we do so, we agree to have our breasts cut open and our hearts and vitals torn from our bodies.'"

This time I did shudder.

"My uncle then declared, 'Behold the chosen three, each born of the Covenant to the sixth generation of our forefather Alonzo Stagg, a most noble Saint, yet who failed in his sacred duty to protect the Prophet Joseph Smith and whose soul cannot rest until the final seed of the great betrayer Thomas Ford is destroyed.'

"We were told to bow our heads while hands from behind us removed the blindfolds. I thought we were to pray. Instead, we stood gazing into an open coffin. It held a skeleton fully clothed in well-worn boots, brown dungarees, a yellowed white shirt with string tie, and a black felt hat. Two candles at each end of the coffin illuminated the scene, their flickering shadows creating an illusion of movement by the bones.

"Denny whispered a prayer and Porter muttered

an oath. Then a voice, deeper even than my uncle's and far more chilling, filled the room.

"'I am the body and suffering spirit of your great-great-grandfather, Alonzo Stagg. I was the Prophet's bodyguard, but failed to protect him from Thomas Ford, who by lies and treachery led Joseph Smith and his brother Hyrum to their martyrdom. For that, I vowed to kill him and for my seed to destroy his seed to the sixth generation. Seven years after the murder of the Prophet, Thomas Ford met his fate at my hand. Thus endeth my part in retribution for my negligence and his great sin.'

"Hands upon our shoulders guided us to the left to gaze into another similarly lit coffin in which lay another skeleton dressed in clothes from a different era. A different voice, higher in tone and less sure of itself, spoke from behind us.

"'I am the earthly remains and heavenly spirit of your great-grandfather Charles Stagg. Of his ten sons by his fifth wife, Martha, I was chosen to continue the sacred weeding of the betrayer's seed. Thomas Ford had two sons and three daughters. The sons became cattle rustlers in Kansas and were caught by vigilantes. The first was tried and hung for his crimes, but the second son attempted to escape. I pulled him from his horse and slit his throat. Thus endeth my part in retribution for my father's negligence and Thomas Ford's great sin.'

"I feared that the bones in the next coffin to be shown would be that of my beloved grandfather. Instead, it was the granduncle to the three of us, a man who had sired twelve children and worn out four wives before dying in bed on top of a fifth. The raspy voice portraying him was that of a brittle old man.

"'I am the earthly remains and heavenly spirit of William Stagg, son of Charles Stagg, grandson of Alonzo Stagg. I was chosen for this sacred duty when my cousin George Reed died of the influenza epidemic. A surviving daughter of Thomas Ford had three children. Julia, the firstborn, died during the same epidemic that took my cousin. Her sister, Katherine, became a Catholic nun. The third was named Louise. She married and produced two male children. I fulfilled my duty by killing the nun as she worked alone in the pantry of her church. Her throat was cut, and her blood spilled upon the ground. Because she was a good and holy woman, I pledged five hundred dollars to our temple in her name and performed the endowment ceremony on her behalf so that she might enter the heavenly kingdom of the Saints.'

"We were turned again to stand in front of an empty coffin, behind which stood Uncle Lamar in his white flannel garments with a cowling over his head. He held a lit candle in one hand and a butcher knife in the other.

"'I am the great-grandson of Alonzo Stagg, grandson of Charles Stagg, and son of Llewellyn Stagg. I was taught in the Danite Bond, initiated into this sacred and most mysterious order by my uncle William. The betrayer Ford's great-granddaughter, Louise, married Bertrand Delaney. They had two children, James and Theodore Delaney. I chose James for atonement, first wounding him with an arrow shot from my bow as he hunted in Alaska's Denali National Forest. I slit his throat and spilled his blood upon the earth. Thus endeth my part in retribution for my great-grandfather's negligence and Thomas Ford's great sin.'"

"There followed another grim tale of assassination, then another turn that completed the circle so that we once again faced the bones of Alonzo Stagg, the man who had uttered the original curse. A dozen hooded men now stood behind his coffin. Each held a candle and a butcher knife. I wondered if my father was among them, but all my instincts told me he would not be part of this cabal. Uncle Lamar spoke for the others.

"'One of you will be called upon to remove the last seed of the betrayer Thomas Ford. His great-great-grandson, Theodore Delaney, has produced a son named Stephen and a daughter Natalie, who is presently ten years of age. The boy is an unsuitable target as he is mentally defective. The girl, however, is healthy and is to be released from this earthly coil upon reaching her majority. The duty entrusted to you is unpleasant but necessary. Should you fail, the efforts of all who have come before will be for naught. Your punishment and shame will attend to you and all your seed.

"'Hear now our decree. Porter Grint, descended from Porter Rockwell, is the chosen avenger. Should he be unable to complete his task because of illness, death, or other circumstances, Dennis Dietz will be called upon. Similarly, Emery Stagg will be Brother Dietz's alternate.

"'Place your hands upon the heart of Alonzo Stagg and take the oath of blood atonement. In so doing, you will purge your ancestor of his shame and free all the Fords, living and dead, of the enmity that has cost them an afterlife in Heaven.'

"We placed our hands on the bony chest and repeated the oath. As if we had a choice."

Chapter 7

Emery, in another breach of Mormon edicts, had been drinking coffee from a thermos bottle all this time and called time-out for a bathroom break. I went over to the counter to see how Josie was faring.

"There was quite a rush for a while," she reported. "Nothing I couldn't handle. You might want to look at the fourteen-volume set of Oscar Wilde's works that Kieran Hennessey brought in. It's the 1908 limited edition signed by Robert Ross. Could be worth something."

No kidding, I thought. Ross, the longtime editor and literary executor for Wilde, had secured the copyrights for the writer's estate and was responsible for resurrecting his literary reputation. This extremely rare set was personally handed out by Ross to four hundred of Wilde's friends at a banquet held eight years after the author's lonely death in Paris. Depending on the condition, it could be worth three thousand dollars.

"Also," she said, "Muldoon wanted to know where you stood on Scottish independence."

"Doesn't he know they voted years ago, and his side lost?"

"Humor him. He's in the medieval section."

"Think I'll take a peek at the Wilde books first," I said.

I had just opened the first volume when Alice Winter charged into the store like a termagant from hell, scattering customers in her wake.

"A word, Bevan! I demand a word with you!"

I rushed from behind the counter.

"What in God's name is the matter?" I whispered, sidling up to her. "You're upsetting the clientele."

"To hell with them. We have to get this settled."

"Get what settled?"

"You know damn well. Your daughter, my son."

Josie appeared then, quietly suggesting that the two of us take our discussion downstairs. This took some of the flame out of Alice's eyes, and after asking Josie to tell Emery I would return shortly, we headed down the stairs.

I'd barely stepped off the last step when Alice snatched me by the collar and stuck her face in mine.

"I told you a month ago that Annie is not to see Mark," she hissed, squeezing the back of my shirt as if it were a noose.

"Then I suggest you tell your son to cancel his trip to Aspen."

This went over as well as you'd expect, leading to a stamping of feet, gnashing of teeth, and everything else short of a dagger in my ribs.

Finally, she calmed down enough for me to get a word in without setting off another eruption.

"You, of all people, know how headstrong my daughter is, Alice. Even if I wanted to interfere—and I don't—she'd never listen to me. Why do you suddenly hate her?"

Alice released her grip and turned away. Her shoulders heaved, and the next thing I heard was an anguished cry. She turned back to me with a look of utter despair.

Impulsively, I took her in my arms, and using her childhood nickname, asked, "What is it, Pigeon? Really? We've been friends far too long for this to come between us."

"You know I could never hate Annie. I'm happy for what she's been able to overcome."

"Then what is it? Is it me?"

She sighed heavily. "In a way, yes." Then, as if coming to a momentous decision, she said, "I don't suppose you've forgotten our last night together."

"When? You mean before I returned to Camp Lejeune? That was nearly a quarter century ago."

"Yes."

"Vaguely," I replied. Then, scanning my memory bank further, said, "It was my last day of holiday leave. I recall our parting was rather bittersweet."

A slow flush crossed her face, and her eyes turned hard.

"That's one way of putting it," she said. "Your Christmas present to me was to say you intended to marry someone else."

I searched her expression for a hint of where she was going with this. I'd thought the matter had been settled long ago. She and my late wife, Carol, had even become friends.

"Yeah. We were both pretty miserable that night."

"Not as miserable as I was."

"It had been a long time coming, Pidge."

"Would you please not call me that anymore?"

"Sorry. But as I recall, you'd been seeing Tim. Our affair was over by then."

Alice looked up at me slyly.

"Not entirely," she said.

No doubt you've already guessed where she was going with this. But you can't imagine the shock I felt. Suddenly, the years peeled away, and I recalled us sitting before a log fire on the veranda of her father's penthouse apartment. A heavy snowstorm had turned the shopping district into a Norman Rockwell postcard. A hundred feet below us, the Spanish-tiled buildings were silhouetted in brightly colored Christmas lights and the sidewalks bustled with thousands of holiday shoppers.

I'd put off giving her the news of my engagement until my final night in Kansas City, and I had brought along a couple of bottles of wine for Dutch courage. Alice and I had been hurling recriminations concerning each other's infidelities throughout the week, but that evening, probably because she sensed what was in the air, it had been like old times when we were just kids who happened to be good friends.

Finally, I put all doubts to rest by telling her of my intent to marry Carol, the daughter of a British colonel I'd met at Camp Lejeune. After an awkward silence, we shared old stories and munched popcorn between voluminous sips of Pinot Noir. It had gone as well as I'd hoped, but when the time came for me to depart, our favorite song, Simply Red's "Holdin' Back the Years," came on the radio.

As has been previously noted, Alice hid a remarkably passionate nature under that wholesome peaches-and-cream exterior. My head was swimming with drink at the time, but I remember how the song had caused us both to blub tears of nostalgia and how she, while heaving those wondrous bosoms, declared how the "new girl" must be wonderful; and how I responded that "she'd have to be to replace you"—which did not help my case in the least because it set the waterworks flowing again—and then we were clutching each other and she reminded me that her father was out of town and—oh, shit!

Math is not my strong suit. But the frantic calculations I performed twenty-some years later in the basement of Riverrun would have put Alan Turing to shame as I counted the months from that last coital union with Alice.

The tyke arrived in September.

She soon confirmed my worst fears. She had discovered she was pregnant with Mark. She told me, the following month—on Martin Luther King Jr. Day, no less! She'd been intimate with Tim before that night, but ever practical, she'd had the foresight to have sex with him on New Year's Eve, ten days after our tryst. It provided a convenient cover for her wedding to him four months later—a shotgun event that her father never forgave poor Winter for supposedly causing.

"Why so sure it was me?" I asked, feeling a curious mixture of shock, incredulity, and delight. After all, it's not every day you wake up to find a twenty-one-year-old son in your bassinette, and I couldn't have found a better one than young Mr.—er—Winter.

"Mark's an only child," Alice answered, "and it's

certainly not from a lack of Tim's efforts—or mine—to have another."

I'd watched Mark grow from a hyperactive little kid through surly adolescence and growing maturity in high school and never noticed a Bevan resemblance. I rarely saw him after he went off to college. But now, recalling the young man I'd seen the previous day at the law school, I'll be damned if it wasn't like looking in a mirror half a lifetime ago. For one thing, he was a couple of inches over six feet, slightly less than my height, but close enough. Then there was that widow's peak and the Bevan floppy earlobes and—Christ! How could I have not connected the dots before?—his feet were at least a size fourteen.

My fraternity brothers hadn't called me "L-Body" for nothing.

"Does he suspect anything?" I asked.

"No one knows except for us. I expect you to keep it that way. Don't even think of attempting a DNA test."

Those last words were accompanied by a glare that would have frozen mercury.

"But that's not fair to either of those kids. They have the right—"

"Screw their rights! The truth is too much for any of us to bear, Mike. Think of what this would do to Tim if he should ever know."

She had a point there. My former law partner wasn't currently on my list of favorite people, but the one thing the Winter marriage had going for it was their deep affection for Mark. Add to that the fact that Tim was the only father—and a damn good one at that—the boy had ever known. Who was I to pull back the curtain from a lifetime of parental devotion and love?

Of course, all this was nothing compared to the effect on our two kids if they actually decided to engage in… Ah, Christ! What a mess.

I gave a little cough. Then raising my chin with the noble gravity of Sydney Carton when he faced the guillotine, said, "All right, Alice. Mum's the word."

"And you'll discourage your daughter from seeing him?"

"Of course. I'll do everything I can, even if it means they both end up hating me."

"Thank you, Mike."

She smiled, patted me on the cheek, and we headed up the stairs.

In response to the puzzled look that Josie gave us, Alice took her by the arm and asked, "Do you suppose Riverrun would be willing to contribute five hundred dollars to the Institute for Noetic Sciences?"

That's Mrs. Winter for you—always on the make for the less fortunate.

Josie knew better than to ask too many questions when it came to the women in my life—it's one of her many fine qualities—and, after ushering Alice out of the shop (with a fifty-dollar check for the institute), she ushered me back to the area where a bladder-relieved Emery Stagg awaited.

Chapter 8

"You look a little peaked," Emery observed, pouring himself another cup of java. After a lifetime of abstinence, the man had clearly become an addict. "Anything wrong?"

"It's nothing, a slight matter of wind. Cabbage for dinner last night."

His eyeballs shifted briefly upward in an expression of bemused sympathy.

Whether it was my sign of discomfort or his relief at being finally able to unload his dark secret to someone besides Natalie, Emery relaxed and became more personable. Before returning to the tale of indoctrination at his uncle's camp, he prattled on about the joys of engineering. Obviously, he was the kind of guy who could no more stem his natural curiosity in science and mechanics that he could stop breathing.

"I remember being five years old," he said, "and wondering how everyday products worked. If something didn't, such as a loose bicycle chain, I looked for the simplest solution to the problem, not stopping until I solved it. I still find myself imagining how I might redesign a toaster or trash compactor to work more effectively. The trouble is that one idea invariably leads to another until my version expands into an entire kitchen or industrial recycling unit. Hours later, I realize I've wasted an entire Sunday on something that will never be produced."

"You must like your job with Becker Systems," I said.

"I do. Certainly, it's more than a paycheck. At least for now. But I can do soil engineering with my eyes closed. My real interest is with fluid dynamics, the physics of geological processes. Dr. Becker lets me fiddle with some open-source programs from time to time. I've created a program that models the complex flows of air and water..."

This went on for an extra ten minutes before the lecture ended with the arrival at the shop of Natalie and her daughter. The girl looked around anxiously but brightened when she saw Josie coming toward the counter with an armful of books.

"It's Princess Claire!" Josie proclaimed, equally happy to see the kid sidling up to help her.

Natalie viewed the warm exchange with barely disguised jealousy, to which the two were oblivious. The pair headed downstairs, and I heard Claire squeal with delight when Josie mentioned having recently seen a fox in our garden.

"'Princess Claire,' my arse," Natalie murmured to herself, shaking her head. Then, noticing Emery and me, she pasted on a smile.

"How's it going, boys? Solved the world's problems yet?"

"Not quite," I said. "Emery was telling me how he and his two cousins got pulled into this blood atonement thing."

"Lamar Stagg was a piece of work, wasn't he?"

Emery frowned at her. "My uncle has his faults, but—"

"Faults? Jesus, the guy is a sadistic nutcase! Why don't you get to the nitty-gritty, Em? I'm going to say goodbye to Claire—that's if Majansik will let me—then I must return to the Center. The cast for the Bloomsday play is coming in to rehearse at three o'clock and I have to get twenty scripts printed. Don't forget to show him the Bible—or whatever the hell it is."

With that, she followed the sounds of Josie and Claire's laughter downstairs.

"Where was I?" Emery asked when she had gone.

"You'd placed your hands on the bones of your ancestor as part of the initiation," I prompted.

"Yeah, thanks." He cleared his throat. "The next day, my aunt returned and surprised us with a party. No mention was made of the ceremony the night before. The cars that had brought the witnesses were gone. After the cake and ice cream, Lamar made a little speech. He was a far different man from the night before. Now, he spoke of love and goodwill, and hoped that Denny and Porter and I would remember the lessons we had learned at the ranch when we went on our foreign missions.

"Taking Regina's hand in his, he blessed us with the wish that we find as good a partner in this life as he had found in his. That afternoon my parents arrived to take me home. Porter, who would be staying behind for another week, didn't see me off, but Denny did. Before leaving, he and I pledged lifelong friendship to each other. We didn't mention the dark vow that bound our souls."

I gave a skeptical look and said, "The fact that you'd pledged to murder a person whose only sin was to carry the DNA of Thomas Ford didn't gnaw at your conscience?"

"Not for a long time. Following a two-year mission in Belize, I entered BYU still convinced that blood atonement was necessary and moral. I'm not proud of it, but it was easier to justify when the odds were slim that I'd be called upon to actually do it."

"I can think of a couple of reasons why it shouldn't have been all that easy," I said. "But I'm one of those cynics who thinks religion causes as many problems as it purports to cure. Of course, anyone who believes that an angel told a poor young farmer in upstate New York where he might dig up a pair of golden plates..."

I let the words hover in the air.

Emery raised his chin defiantly. "Get this straight," he said with a dry, insistent voice. "I may drink coffee and beer, and I haven't seen the inside of an LDS temple in over a year, but I still consider myself a Mormon. Only now I look to the parables—call it the mythology—for spiritual guidance, not literal truth."

I looked at him without saying anything, which merely goaded him on.

"How is it that perfectly open-minded people such as you feel free to make snide remarks about the Mormon faith? You ridicule our temperate habits, particularly when it comes to caffeine, booze, and chastity before marriage. You mock the names we give our children. We're labeled non-Christian because we don't acknowledge the cross as a symbol, finding its emphasis on intense suffering to not be a particularly wholesome thing. And you excoriate our holy book as the work of a bankrupt con man rather than a charismatic saint on a par with the greatest disciples."

"My apologies," I said. "But you pride yourself on your rational thinking. You're an engineer, for heaven's sake. How can you or anyone accept spirit weddings, after-death baptisms of everyone from Stalin to Walt Disney, multiple gods each with his own universe—"

"Hold on a second," Emery interrupted. "I've heard that, in one form or another, from every gentile I've ever known, including Natalie." He clasped his hands and leaned toward me.

"I assume you were raised Catholic," he said.

"I still attend Mass on Christmas Eve and Easter."

"Then you ascribe to the virgin birth of Christ?"

"Uhh. Let's just say I don't put that on a par with the Resurrection."

Emery smiled at my hypocrisy.

"Joseph Smith told a crowd in Nauvoo that he didn't blame anyone for not believing his history. If he hadn't experienced it, he would have found it fanciful himself. But, you see, the Prophet believes he did live it, and despite all the disparagement his words have received from doubters, Smith created a religion that has not only survived, but become the fastest-growing church in America. And as for those gold plates, I seem to recall Moses was handed a couple of stone tablets right after his chat with a burning bush."

"Point taken," I said, seeing no reason for either of us to try and convert the other. My respect for him had grown in the last few minutes, while at the same time I was feeling ashamed of my snide and disdainful attitude toward his religion. Still, I wasn't about to drop the subject of blood atonement.

"When did you begin to question your uncle's dictates?"

"After I graduated from college. But it was more from practical reasons than a shift in ideology. The challenges of making a living pushed my commitment into the background. I took a job with a water treatment firm in San Jose and for the first time in my life associated with gentiles. Finding their less judgmental ways to be refreshing, I even dated a Presbyterian. It's not that she was a real girlfriend—I suspect Helen hung out with me because I could fix her computer—but she was kind. Inevitably, I began to associate her with the girl we had pledged to kill. I began to question what Lamar had programmed us for."

"But you still weren't prepared to prevent it?"

Emery edged forward in his chair. "No. I just prayed to God that the retribution wouldn't fall on my shoulders. Then, shortly after my twenty-eighth birthday, Porter Grint was convicted of second-degree manslaughter for stabbing a man to death in Rock Springs. A Wyoming jury sentenced him to twenty years."

"So the torch passed to Dennis Dietz."

The bland mask returned. "Yes. But we hadn't been in touch for years, so I didn't know if Denny had become as uncomfortable with the pledge as I had. It didn't matter though. Much to our uncle's dismay, Denny had become a Marine officer. Six months after Porter's appeal was denied, he was wounded during his second tour in Afghanistan. The former surfing champ returned alive, but not whole—a Mon-50 directional fragmentation mine had taken both legs, his right arm, and his right eye."

"How soon did you hear from your uncle?"

"He called to tell me a week after he'd learned of it. Almost as an afterthought, Lamar added that a 'certain young lady' had lived long past her majority. He didn't have to remind me of my obligation, but he could tell by the hesitancy in my voice that I lacked commitment. I was summoned to Colorado."

"If you had doubts, why didn't you simply refuse to go?"

Emery rubbed his jaw. He was silent a moment, then he said slowly, carefully, "The oath was implanted in my brain, wiring my will to its dictates. Despite my lax church attendance, I was no apostate. Either Brigham Young and Joseph Smith were prophets of God or they were not. Either Alonzo Stagg and his descendants were vengeance-seeking monsters, or they were avenging angels selected to right a terrible wrong."

He ignored the appalled look on my face and pressed on.

"All that I had been taught to believe was that the doctrine of blood atonement was moral and necessary. The very principles of Mormon eternity were at stake. I intended to confront my uncle with my doubts, to see if he might have reinterpreted the doctrine."

I knew little about cults, let alone brainwashing. But I understood from my own experience how easy it is to deceive oneself, no matter how crackpot the rationalization. What a person wishes to be true, no matter how crazy, he usually finds a way to believe until a better option comes along.

"Lamar was seventy-five when I arrived at the

lodge," Emery continued. "And suffered from emphysema, but the holy fire in his eyes had not dimmed. His long, once-powerful body slumped in a reclining chair. Although he was next to a roaring fire in the great stone hearth, a thick wool Pendleton blanket covered his legs. Without so much as a greeting to me when I entered the room, he recited Brigham Young's decree:

"'All mankind love themselves…and yet he would be glad to have his blood shed. That would be loving themselves, even unto an eternal exaltation. Will you love your brothers and sisters likewise, when they have committed a sin that cannot be atoned for without the shedding of their blood? Will you love that man or woman well enough to shed their blood?'"

"And still you didn't walk away?"

Emery shook his head. Avoiding my eyes, he picked up the *Book of Mormon* from the table. In a droning voice, as if, once again, he was talking to himself, he said, "This, my very blood, spoke to me, dissolving all will. I redeclared my affirmation. My core belief had been tested, and it was not found wanting. It was as if the angel Moroni himself had spoken to me. In dispatching the Ford descendant, I would save her from everlasting torment. The mad reasoning behind the oath was that it rationalized murder as a charitable act. Compounding the insanity was the understanding that if I failed to act, all the other killings would have been in vain. It was on this that I reaffirmed my vow."

He returned the *Book of Mormon* to the table. This time he looked at me. A muscle twitched in his cheek as he continued.

"Lamar planted a kiss on my forehead and said, 'This ends with you. You shall be exalted by the

brother his trespasses standeth condemned before the Lord; for there remaineth in him the greater sin.

"'Ten. I, the Lord, will forgive whom I will forgive, but of you, it is required to forgive all men.'

"At first I wondered if Lamar intended to retract everything he'd said about blood atonement. But he wasn't one to mince words or speak in riddles—nor was he likely to experience a crisis of faith, as misbegotten as it might be. Aunt Regina was dying of throat cancer. Maybe that had something to do with it. But why couldn't he tell me it was no longer necessary or moral to comply with the oath? I wanted a definitive answer."

"Did you get it?"

Emery rubbed the back of his neck. "I tend to overanalyze and dwell on the internal architecture, whether it's a machine or person. But I don't think emotions are bad impulses to be suppressed lest they get in the way of rational thinking. The next morning Lamar called to tell me Regina had died. There was no mention of blood atonement. I thought my prayers had been answered."

At that moment, Natalie returned from downstairs. She was smiling again. Apparently, the differences with Josie had been resolved.

"What prayer was answered this time?" Natalie asked.

"I was telling him about my aunt's passing."

"Oh." She turned to me. "That same day Emery came to Café Provence to give me a rose he'd plucked from his garden."

"And to invite you to the funeral," Emery said.

"Oh, yes. That. I was astounded, especially when he said the service would be somewhere in the Rocky

Mountains. Until then, he was just a customer, a quiet one at that. The encounter behind my house was the first time I'd seen him outside the bistro and here he was inviting me to meet his relatives at his aunt's burial."

"You laughed at me," Emery reminded her.

"Not at you," Natalie said, chuckling, "but the absurdity of your request. I mean, I've been invited on some weird dates, but to a funeral?"

"It worked," he said, tossing a gentle smile at her.

"What worked?" I asked.

"I knew I'd have to do something audacious to attract her attention," he explained. "For engineers, fear of failure is the biggest cause of inaction. But I have a theory that it's really failure only if you don't learn from it, so…"

"Have I mentioned Emery has a highly developed frontal cortex?" Natalie said suggestively. "Just what every girl desires in a man."

Emery tilted his head questioningly. So did I.

I wasn't sure anymore where the jokes ended and nutty reality began. Leaving aside the fact that Emery had come to town to cut her throat, Natalie, who could have had her pick of men, seemed totally captivated by a person who had about as much charm as the mathematical equation for terminal velocity. I wondered, not for the first time: Was her ardor an act?

"There I was," she said, jumping back into the story, "trying to figure out how to say 'Hell no' nicely when he hands me the rose. It was a brilliant move. I take it, of course, and immediately find myself stabbed by a thorn. My thumb is spurting quarts of blood, I'm hopping around the tables, and I drop my order pad into a customer's crème brûlée. I started guffawing so loud that snot flew out of my nose onto Em's shirt. Every eye in the place was staring at us by then.

"Once the giggles subsided," she said, grasping Emery's hand, "I thought, 'Oh, what the hell?' So I tested him. I said I'd go but that he'd have to take Claire, too. I thought for sure that would be a deal breaker without hurting his feelings."

"Was it?" I asked.

Emery looked surprised that I would think such a thing. "Of course it was okay by me. More than okay. We had a wonderful time with the family. Even Uncle Lamar was charmed by them."

With that bit of extraordinary news, he handed me the *Book of Mormon* and closed the briefcase. I gave him a receipt, evidence that he had lent me the inscribed Palmyra edition, then shouted downstairs to tell Josie our guests were leaving.

She and Claire soon joined us at the front door. The pale-haired child was upbeat as she described to me in her forthright manner one of the three books she carried in the crook of her arm.

It was *Irish Earth Folk* by Diarmuid MacManus, an odd book that claimed certain woods, meadows, and bogs of Ireland were haunted by fairies and leprechauns, all fallen angels of one sort or another.

"They are powerful spirits to be treated with respect," she said, staring into my eyes.

In that instant, she was no longer a child, but an all-knowing sibyl, a wise woman of indeterminate age, who seemed to know all my secrets. Sensing my discomfort, she smiled as if to reassure me. Then she was a girl again, walking after her mother and Emery into an overcast day.

As much as I wanted to believe Emery had

forsaken his macabre oath, I couldn't help but think that the only catalyst leading him to reject blood atonement was his infatuation for Natalie. What would happen should he ever tire of her?

Or to the strange child named Claire?

Chapter 9

"So what do you think of that girl?" Josie asked over Irish coffee the next morning. We were outside, on our little patio at home, reading the newspapers.

"Claire's okay," I answered evasively. "A little goofy, but what kid isn't at that age? She seems to cheer up when she's around you. Why?"

Josie looked around, pausing, careful in her response. "I really think there's something unusual about her. Have you noticed how when stressed, she constantly combs her hair?"

I hadn't, but lots of things women do escape me. After mentioning Natalie's concern about Claire, I went back to perusing the latest Royals' batting averages.

"Are you listening?"

"Uh-huh," I mumbled and kept reading.

"She was hanging around in the science section yesterday, and I had my usual chat with her. At one point, she asked if she could keep one of the mice she'd spotted in the storeroom."

"Mice!" I exclaimed, nearly spilling my drink on the box scores.

I may have overreacted, but ever since a customer told me that my former barista fed rats (he referred to them as "Irish chipmunks") on the back steps of River-run, I've been more than a little sensitive about rodents —and baristas. The glue used in old tomes is tastier than cheese to the vermin, and an entire library could be destroyed overnight by a pack of them. Since then, I'd developed a nice relationship with a local pest control service. That is, as nice as one can have with twice-a-month visits at two hundred dollars a pop.

"How many critters did she see?"

"Seven, but she wisely noted that could change quickly since two seemed pregnant," Josie said. "She expressed surprise that we hadn't noticed them, since it was obvious to her. Then she shrugged and turned away, pulling back into her shell.

"She's a strange mixture of fragility and strength, Michael, and I'd somehow alienated her. I suggested that we go to the park for some fresh air, and she readily agreed. When we got there, I started pointing out birds and other critters."

Josie took a sip of coffee, watching for my reaction. Fortunately, I resisted the urge to roll my eyes. She was always pointing out wildlife, whether in our yard, while jogging, or hauling groceries to our car. It was one of those goofy little things Josie did that I found in equal parts endearing and annoying. If I had a nickel for every blue jay, junco, cardinal, wren, hawk, owl, and woodpecker that she urged me to notice, I'd be a rich man. Even richer if you want to count the bugs, butterflies, dragonflies, and other creatures. But I smiled knowingly and nodded for her to continue.

"Claire felt comfortable with me after that and began identifying birds that I failed to notice, even an owl that was perfectly camouflaged in a giant pin oak. It was stunning how she beat me at my own game."

Josie was really worked up recalling the girl's uncanny affinity for wildlife, but I had yet to see where this appreciation was headed.

"Claire wasn't just pointing them out, Michael; she was communing with them. She'd make this little trilling noise or nod her head or give a little chirp, depending on the species and the creatures' responses. I've never seen a child have such awareness. It was more than being a skilled birdwatcher or a budding naturalist."

"Granted," I said. "She has unusual vibes. Ask anyone at the Celtic Center who saw her weird act before O'Halloran collapsed. But so what?"

"It's more than just being different or supersensitive," Josie insisted. "Claire's plugged into life in a way that's different from everybody else. Consider her calming influence among the dying at the assisted living center, her otherworldly singing voice, the constant combing. Even her appearance."

"Okay?" I asked, still befuddled.

Her voice lowered. "Claire Phelan thinks she's a banshee."

This time I did spill my coffee. "What?"

"This isn't entirely my idea," Josie said. "Natalie told me that her pet name for Claire used to be 'my little banshee baby,' because of the way she howled when she had to go to bed. The kid started to believe it and went around trying to tame opossums, raccoons, bunnies and any other critters she encountered in the parks. It escalated when Claire was six or seven and began reading up on the faeries—that old book of Irish folktales she bought here the other day was far from the first on the subject. Only lately, however, has Natalie noticed that she has ramped up her fantasies, claiming connections to eerie things most people don't see."

"I thought the traditional bean se, or banshee, came in the form of a shrieking old woman."

"Nope, that's the Hollywood version, making them witchlike. Originally, banshees were thought to be part human and part faeries. They can be young or aged, beautiful or decayed. And here's another weird thing—they have a great fondness for linen."

I remembered how Claire enjoyed doing laundry at the assisted living home.

"There's more. Irish legend says that because of their connection to the spirit world, banshees can tell when death is approaching. They are death messengers, ghostly female heralds who exist to guide the departed to the other world with their shrill cries."

Josie paused, frowning at my look of skepticism. "All I know is that Claire is differently tuned in to nature, and that she believes she has some kind of gift. Or curse. Facts, Michael. Be aware that we need to keep an eye on this kid. That's all I'm saying."

"Do you think she could help Feklar?" I asked with a wicked grin. "Maybe she can whisper to the demon cat about the litter box—"

I stopped when Josie slugged me on the arm.

"I know this sounds a little crazy," she said.

"A little?"

I stood and stretched. The brilliantly clear sky was the color of the Swede's shirt, as they say in the Midwest. I was about to go in when I saw a hawk zoom across our yard. At least, I think it was a hawk.

Chapter 10

Luck whines, labor whistles.

I wish I could remember who said that. Had to be Marty Meeks, the same self-righteous prig who scribbled "Good, better, best; never let them rest, until the good is better and the better best" in my high school yearbook. (Last I looked on Facebook, Marty had announced he was leaving his service manager position at Jiffy Lube for "another calling.")

I don't care whether it whines, whistles, or farts; I'll always take luck—the good kind, anyway—over drudgery and toil. Emery Stagg's *Book of Mormon* could sell for a cool quarter million dollars, perhaps more. That meant a hefty commission for Riverrun.

But, as I've often noticed, once you answer good fortune's knock, prepare for the door to slam on your ass after it crosses the portal. The trick is to hedge your bet while the cards are still hot so that when the inevitable turn comes you land on a goose-down mattress. My plan was to increase the benefits of this windfall by asking Eulalia Darp to assist with the sale rather than try to sell it myself. Not only would her reputation attract higher bidders for the book, but her gratitude for gaining a share of the commission might also assure my admittance to the ABAA. And that meant a gold ticket to future success in the antiquarian business.

Even so, offering to split fees was counterintuitive. I figured it wouldn't hurt to get some objective advice.

Only not from Josie.

As much as I trusted her judgment, she had a funny notion that overreaching—whether picking apples or grabbing front-row seats—was rarely wise, often impolite, and sometimes unethical.

After explaining to her that I needed to prepare a set of books for shipping, I descended to the basement storeroom, where I locked the door behind me. Then I opened the steel filing cabinet and brought out the bag.

It felt somewhat heavier than when I'd last carried it to the table a month earlier. I attributed that to the feeling that had grown ever since returning with it from Ivo Mackin's mountain Shangri-La—namely, that it had been a tad improper, if not illegal, to remove the mummified head of Captain James Cook from where it had lain for centuries in a cave high above Kealakekua Bay. But the great eighteenth-century explorer had no heirs, and I figured I had as much right to it as modern-day Hawaiians whose ancestors had murdered, cannibalized, and kept what was left of him in a basket there.

Putting those thoughts to rest, I lifted the muslin cloth and proceeded to consult with a mentor who was not only wise, but more practical than a priest—or Josie—when it came to questions of conscience.

Funny how madness creeps on you. You see, Claire Phelan wasn't the only one a little touched by the faeries. I'd spent yesterday morning snidely confronting Emery for his belief in angels and multiple heavens, and this morning expressing amazement hearing about a girl who thought she was a banshee. Yet here I was seeking wisdom from the spirit of a man who had been murdered more than two hundred fifty years ago.

WHEN I RETURNED UPSTAIRS twenty minutes later, Josie was waiting with crossed arms and a faint, quizzical smile. Her tongue played with the inside of her cheek.

She began slowly. "Sooo…what were you doing down there?"

I pretended not to hear while looking past her at the happy-hour crowd streaming into Café Provence. The late afternoon sun broke through the clouds with shafts of silver and gold, highlighting the hair of the women. It reminded me of something Yeats had written:

…She who had brought great Hector down

And put all Troy to wreck…

"Michael?"

I returned my gaze to her. "Yes, love?"

"I heard you talking to yourself in your secret lair."

"It's not secret."

"It is when you lock the door. So what's with the yakking to walls?"

"Just a habit I've developed when wrapping books."

"Since when?"

"Since New Zealand. I'm working through some issues."

"Is paranoia one of them?"

"Josie, please. It's nothing like that. I'm fine. Lots of people talk to themselves."

"Oh, yeah? Like who?"

"Bobo Jenkins whenever he crashes into a ruck."

"Your rugby pals don't count." She uncrossed her arms and began tapping her fingers on the counter. "You addressed the person as 'Captain' and were answering questions as well as asking them."

"Was I?"

"Don't fuck with me, Bevan."

Natalie Phelan wasn't the only one with a temper.

"It's a quirk I've developed to address some issues."

"What issues?"

"Nothing major. Something to help get me through the day."

"Oh," she said sarcastically. "Is that all? I was under the impression that things were going pretty well for us."

"They are, Josie."

I put my arms around her and whispered in her ear. "What say we close for the day to celebrate the *Book of Mormon* deal? Maybe shake a few rafters in our bedroom."

She pulled away. "Don't change the subject! I'm more worried about you than Claire."

"No need to be concerned."

"Then who's the captain?"

Time to come clean. Sort of.

"Ever see the movie *Harvey*?" I asked.

"Yeahhh…" she answered. "Jimmy Stewart talks to an imaginary six-foot rabbit who wears a bow tie.

People think he's nuts—Stewart's character, not the rabbit."

"Right. But he isn't. It's what keeps him sane, conversing with his id or something."

"Like the relationship little girls have with their dolls?"

"Or Claire's fixation with banshees. C'mon, Josie. Try to be serious for a change. The Celts have a long-standing tradition of putting trust in shape-shifting spirits. Superstition is in my DNA."

"Well, thank God you only have your chats in the storeroom. You do, don't you?"

"Of course. D'ya think I'm crazy?"

She tilted her head, shut one eye, scrunched up her nose while considering the question. Then, "So what advice did this captain give you—if it's not too personal?"

Think fast, Bevan.

"He said I should marry you before you get cold feet."

She stared ahead for a moment. A couple of heart-beats later, the gray-green eyes turned soft and the corners of her mouth slanted upward.

"Okay, Michael, you're off the hook for now. Let's go see about those rafters."

And that, for all practical purposes, ended the interrogation on a high note.

Chapter 11

Stormin' Norman Tate was perched on a ladder, dabbing gold leaf on a carved sunburst above Eulalia's front door when I arrived the next morning. Daisy, the golden retriever, sat by the lower rung, observing the flicking of Tate's wrists as if it were a magical human ritual. So entranced was she that my sudden presence on the porch was barely acknowledged.

"Back for more punishment?" Tate asked, gazing over his shoulder.

"I have something to show Miss Darp."

He made a final delicate stroke with the tiny brush, then stepped off the ladder.

"It'd best be a book."

"It is. A very important religious book."

He looked dubious. "Hope it ain't one of them German doorstops."

I knew what he meant. Every family in the Midwest seemed to have a nineteenth-century Bible they believed an illustrious ancestor had brought over from the old country. In fact, most had been printed in Philadelphia by Globe Publishing or the A.J. Holman Company. Called "Salesman Bibles" because the samples were sold door-to-door, their features included Gothic Fraktur typeface, brass clasps on heavy leather boards, and a ten-inch Teutonic cross with a sparkly crown on a deteriorating front. Inside these three-to-five-pound tomes (depending on whether the New Testament was included with the Old), woodblock engravings depicted sword-wielding archangels putting paid in full to cringing demons and apostates alike. You can get a pretty good copy on eBay for fifteen dollars.

"Nope," I replied. "And I haven't drowned any ducks in the past twenty-four hours."

That got a chuckle.

"All right. But it best be good as you say, 'cuz she's crankier than usual today. That's why I'm outside findin' other things to do. You go right on in. Last I noticed, she be in the back galley eatin' lunch."

Norman climbed back on the ladder and I went through the living room, past the staircase, and into a small, utilitarian kitchen—original wood cabinets, linoleum floor, old refrigerator, older stove. Eulalia sat at a battered round oak table almost hidden beneath a disorderly pile of ledgers and billing statements. I entered just as she spooned hominy from a tin can directly into her mouth. I apologized for the intrusion, but she seemed unperturbed, even pleased to see me.

"That didn't take long," she said, looking at the book in my hand. She put down the spoon and wiped her mouth with a paper napkin. "What have you brought me?"

I handed her the *Book of Mormon*.

"Palmyra?"

"Yes," I said. "Inscribed by Sidney Rigdon to Alonzo Stagg."

She raised her eyebrows, peered over her spectacles at me, and opened the book.

"So it would seem," she confirmed after a cursory look at the frontispiece. "Who owns it?"

"A local man named Emery Stagg. It's an heirloom with a direct line of provenance."

"Is he prepared to sell it?"

"Depends on the offer."

"But why bring it here when you've got one of the foremost collectors of Mormon materials in nearby Independence? Delbert Hander recently paid a hundred and fifty thousand dollars for an LDS hymnal."

"True," I agreed, "but he's tapped out because of it. Anyway, Delbert doesn't have influence with the ABAA."

She smiled very faintly. "Be that as it may, I'm in my waning years, Mr. Bevan. Even if I were interested, I'm not in a position to spend that kind of money."

"Perhaps," I suggested, glancing at the pile of invoices at her elbow. "You might spread the word among your contacts. Rather than take it directly for auction at Swann's or Heritage, I'm willing to share some of my commission with you. Say twenty-five percent?"

She knew from the first moment I entered her kitchen that I would offer something of that nature. Protocol, however, required that I tap-dance first so it wouldn't look like she was seeking a bribe to support my ABAA application.

"I suppose I could mention it to Ken Sanders in Salt Lake." She withdrew a pencil from behind her ear.

"Or Henry Weiss in Phoenix. There are plenty of potential buyers in Mormon country eager for memorabilia of the early founders. If the inscription is real, it should create a bidding frenzy."

"I assure you it is, Eula."

"Do you, indeed? Since I'm not an expert on Mormon-abilia, you can understand my concern. Leave this with me so I can have the archivist at the Spencer Library confirm its authenticity. Then I'll begin making calls to my colleagues. Really, it's the only way, my boy."

Seeing my hesitation, she squeezed the pencil between thumb and forefinger and reached for an unopened envelope. "Spell your name," she said. "Mustn't get it wrong in my letter to the ABAA."

"It's B-e-v-a-as-in-apple-n."

"Thank you." She finished writing my name and then said, "I also accept your generous offer to split the commission fifty-fifty."

"Split? But I said—"

I stopped in mid-sentence, remembering what the legendary Frances Steloff once said of herself: "You can't be an angel and be a purveyor of books."

Chapter 12

Eulalia Darp telephoned me at Riverrun three days later with good news.

"Spencer Library confirmed the book is legitimate and remarkably significant," she told me. "I've spoken to half a dozen other dealers who have interested buyers. In fact, Marty Lowe in Santa Clara has a client so eager that the man is flying in tomorrow to inspect it."

"What's his name?"

"Marty wouldn't say. The client doesn't want word to get out that he's interested until he's had a chance to look at the book. He also insisted on meeting you."

"When does he arrive at your place?"

"Four thirty."

"See you then."

It was one of those midsummer evenings in the Midwest when all the world's problems seem far away. Neighborhood kids played kickball in the yard next door as Josie and I settled on our patio to share a bottle of Two Paddocks wine. A massive blue moon rose above a line of sycamore trees illuminating a sky as clear as Saint Augustine's conscience, but it soon became apparent that clouds had gathered in my true love's heart.

"Hey, Bevan."

"Yes, darling?"

"Concerning what you said the other day, were you serious?"

"The other day? Serious? Let me see." I began to sense mischief, but for the life of me, I hadn't a clue what she was referring to. A thought occurred, however. "Oh, yes. I'll definitely see to the brake pads. Don't want to slam into the back of a bus. Better safe than—"

"This is not about your Jeep."

And suddenly I remembered. To bluster would be a waste of time, hoisted as I had been on my own petard in a moment's weakness.

"I was only joking," I lied. "About the brakes, I mean. I'm thinking sometime—"

"Soon."

"Yes. Next—"

"This."

"Right. This September. In Aspen. Romantic enough for you?"

"Yeah," she said with only the slightest hint of suspicion. "That would be great."

"How does the third weekend of the month sound?"

Josie checked the calendar app on her cell phone, then looked at me sideways. "Ohhhh, I see. You want us to get married during the Aspen Ruggerfest?"

"The Blues need an inside center and invited me to try out. C'mon, think of it as mixing business with pleasure."

"Cripes, Bevan! I know which you think is the business end of it. You're the last of the great romantics. How could I be so lucky?" She reached for her wineglass.

"It's a great time of the year to be there, when the aspen leaves are turning gold and there's the first snow in the high summits and—what do you say? Let's be different."

"I don't mind sharing our wedding with your rugby mates, but we will not do it at halftime with you getting blood and mud all over my dress. I saw what happened to Sammy Riegle's poor bride."

The woman knew how to drive a hard bargain.

"Following the match then?" I suggested. "I'll even shower."

With that, Josie put down her glass, sat on my lap, and stuck her tongue halfway down my throat.

I took that for a "yes."

Later we were cuddling before the TV set when a news flash came on showing a raging fire engulf a stately Victorian home. Kids from the nearby fraternities and sororities were shown frenziedly passing buckets of water to prevent the blaze from spreading to their houses.

The perky blond reporter from Channel 9 was in her mid-twenties and obviously cherishing the opportunity—nothing like a deadly fire near a popular college campus to boost ratings, not to mention a career that, heretofore, had consisted mostly of post-robbery interviews at convenience stores.

"The owner of the residence is—was—noted antique book expert Eulalallia… er…Eulyia Darp. Her body was found in her upstairs bedroom. The other body was found near the front door of the Victorian-style landmark. It appears to be that of a Native American male, although preliminary identification is difficult due to the charred remains…"

The coverage concluded with a shot of Daisy, the golden retriever, being held back by a stunned young man wearing a Sigma Chi T-shirt. I spotted the burly figure of Buford Higgins in the background. He was wearing the porkpie hat that was two sizes too small and a disgusted look on his face.

"Reporting from the scene in Lawrence, Kansas, this is Janie Bustermann with 'News You Can Use.'"

Josie and I looked at each other in stunned silence. Then, after spending the better part of ten minutes commiserating for the victims and contemplating the fickle finger of fate, it was Josie who was the first to come to grips with how the tragedy would affect us.

"You'll have to find someone else to support your application to the ABAA."

"Right," I agreed miserably. "But, uh, there's something else, Josie. Something I should have run by you first."

"Why are you trembling, Michael?"

"It seems Emery's *Book of Mormon* may have perished with the victims."

"I don't understand…"

"I lent it to her."

"You *what?*"

I hastily tried to explain why, but it only made matters worse, particularly when I admitted I'd forgotten to get a receipt for the book from Eulalia.

Josie let out her breath, got to her feet, and like Banquo's ghost, silently ascended the stairs.

I settled on the couch with Feklar the demon cat for what promised to be yet another sleepless night.

Chapter 13

The next morning, I found a subdued Josie and an exhausted me in Lawrence gaping over yellow police tape at the still-smoldering pile of blackened timbers and scorched skeletal walls.

Slushy pockets of soot covered the floor. A noisy generator pumped hundreds of gallons from the basement through a thick canvas and rubber hose, creating a gray-black river of slime down Tennessee Street. The acrid reek from smoldering plastic wires, PVC pipes, and asbestos insulation created a dangerous cocktail of hydrogen chloride, carbon dioxide, and other toxins. Most of the walls and part of the staircase continued to harbor caught gasses and active smoke.

Periodically, a shift of the wind brought the stench of roasted flesh.

The grand old house had survived Quantrill's raid in 1863, only to succumb to this ignoble end.

Among the rubble of smoldering furniture, rugs, and piles of insulation lay shattered vases, lamps, and stained glass. Then there were the books. Thousands of charred, water-sodden volumes. All of them distinctive. Dozens so rare as to be irreplaceable.

Smoke that had been free-floating during the fire had settled as a dusty film on what remained of the library-style tables and other horizontal surfaces. Above the marble fireplace mantel sat two chunks of melted lead; sad remnants of the dancing harlequin bookends. In the space between them, only water-sodden ashes remained of Huckleberry Finn, The Red Badge of Courage, and other first-state, first-edition American classics.

A dozen investigators wearing nitrile rubber gloves, chemical-resistant coveralls, boots, helmets with glass visors, and respirator tanks waded among the debris sifting for evidence with tiny metal rakes. One of them spent a considerable time poking around the couch that Eulalia had sat on during my visit. It was a mess of blackened springs and charred casters, but he seemed to have found something interesting enough to place in his basket.

Another investigator searched for anything remotely salvageable. The task seemed hopeless, but he was diligent. After twenty minutes, he had filled a straw-lined plastic milk box. Josie and I followed him to a table set up on the lawn of the Sigma Chi house, where an attractive middle-aged woman wearing a full-body apron used a dry-cleaning sponge to wipe off a huge sheet of parchment.

"Put them on the stand over there," the woman ordered. "I don't want them near what I'm working on."

After the investigator had done as told and returned to the rubble, Josie and I introduced ourselves to the restorer.

"I know you," she said, continuing to concentrate on her task. "You're the owners of Riverrun Books. Nice shop. I'm Renata Wormington, chief archivist at the Spencer Library."

"Have you come across a *Book of Mormon*?" I asked.

"The inscribed Palmyra edition?"

"Yes."

She shook her head. "I authenticated it for Miss Darp. Was it yours?"

"In a manner of speaking," Josie answered for me.

We watched while she dabbed water off the colored linen threads of the sheet containing a pair of sparrow hawks drawn in the unmistakable style of John James Audubon.

"Is that what I think it is?" I asked.

"Yup," she said, reaching for a blow dryer. She set it on low and held the warm air briefly over a brightly illustrated tail feather. "From *Birds of America*. It's not from the 1838 first—there are only a hundred twenty left of the original two hundred printed—but Eulalia owned the 1844 edition. All eight volumes of the double-elephant folio set. Plenty rare enough. The entire set would have fetched over a million dollars. I always told her she shouldn't keep them in the house. But then that would apply to most of her collection."

"Where are the rest of the plates? I thought Audubon produced over four hundred of them."

She shut off the dryer and looked up at me.

"Actually, there were four hundred thirty-five, done in eighty-seven sets of five. It took him thirteen years to portray just about every gorgeous bird on the continent."

She turned the sheet over and returned to her task. "This is a triage station, Mr. Bevan. I've sent sixteen plates to the university lab for flash freezing and further restoration. As for the rest, what the fire didn't destroy the water hoses did. There are no more that can be salvaged. Excuse me…"

Seeing that her eyes had filled with tears, we quietly withdrew.

I'd like to think the blubbering was for the loss of a dear colleague and not for a bunch of bird pictures. But I wouldn't bet on it.

Of course, I was no better. As appalled as I was at the tragic death of two people I'd just met and the destruction of books worth several fortunes, I couldn't help but ponder the devastating effect this event would have on the future of Riverrun. It wasn't just a door that had slammed on us, but an eighteen-ton steel grate. There was no way Emery Stagg's *Book of Mormon* could have survived that inferno. And there was no way our bookstore would ever prosper unless Emery had thought to insure his treasure.

The odds of that? About a zillion to one.

My mind raced with other ways to recover the loss. Eulalia would surely have had insurance, but aside from her not being around to collect it, Emery's *Book of Mormon* was not hers to claim.

As a lawyer, I'd been required to carry malpractice insurance. Booksellers can voluntarily obtain a policy for "Errors and Omissions," but few do. It's usually not worth it in a business where most screw-ups are settled with an apology and the offer of future trade credit.

Even if I'd bothered to get a policy, however, it wouldn't have covered my actions. More than a simple error, more than malpractice, I had intentionally entrusted a valuable heirloom to another party without obtaining permission from the owner. And why? So I could piggyback on the fame of someone with a better resume than mine. Now, because I'd been too eager to impress Eulalia Darp with the hope of gaining entrance to the ABAA, my carefully rehabilitated reputation would once again be in tatters.

It was on the long, silent ride back to Lawrence with Josie at the wheel that I found the courage to call Emery.

"Hi, Mike. Any news on what we might be offered for the book?"

"Nothing good."

"I don't understand. Few bidders?"

"There aren't going to be any bidders."

Silence at his end, followed by my painful three-minute monologue about the fire and the loss of his heirloom.

"You lent my valuable property to someone without my permission?" His voice was a flat, hollow whisper.

"It was for your benefit. At least it seemed so. I'm sorry, Emery. Miss Darp is—was—one of the world's most respected bibliophiles. Her support meant a vast increase in the number of viable offers."

"Where are you?"

"Driving back from Lawrence."

"I'll see you at your shop."

He hung up.

Emery and Natalie stood in front of Riverrun when we arrived. They looked like the couple in Grant Wood's painting American Gothic—only not as cheerful.

I unlocked the door in silence and the four of us settled in the wingback chairs in the philosophy section.

"Didn't you say you could get two hundred for it? Possibly more." Emery posed it as a statement, not a question. He was on a short fuse.

"Yes."

"What about the rest?"

"I don't understand."

"Pain and suffering for the loss."

"This isn't a personal injury case," the lawyer in me answered.

A spasm of rage gripped his throat. "You knew how much this meant to us. You as much as lied to me when you loaned the book to someone without my permission. There must be a penalty for that kind of fraud."

Natalie put her hand on Emery's wrist. Her face was a white mask. She looked at me with doleful eyes.

"We don't mean to be greedy," she said. "But you'd set our hopes so high. Then to lose it all…it was to be our new beginning."

"Believe me, I understand. We have the resources to make it up to you. But it will take a little time."

Disgusted by my offer, Emery started to get up, only to have Natalie push him back down.

"We've got to be practical, Em. Listen to what Mike has to say."

The engineer's eyes still smoldered, but when he next spoke, the scold in his voice was replaced by resignation.

"When would there have been an auction if things had gone right?"

"Three or four months if we were to go through a major auction house. Possibly sooner if a solo buyer came up with a substantial offer."

"All right," he said, all business now. "You have

until November to come up with two hundred thousand dollars. Otherwise, I'll advise Tim Winter to file suit."

Lovely. Tim was not only the husband of Alice and purportedly faux father of Mark, he was my old law partner. He had pulled strings to reinstate my law license, but when I refused his offer to join his firm in order to revive Riverrun, our friendship turned as cold as his surname.

We all rose at the same time. Natalie reached for Josie's arm after Emery stalked through the door.

"I'm so sorry this has happened," I heard Natalie say to her. "It's not just the money. Of all the people we know in this town, you were the ones who I—we— thought could be trusted."

More than the humiliation of being caught using another dealer to handle the sale, more than the catastrophic amount we owed having lost the book, it was this last accusation that cut deepest.

For the time being, anyway.

No use dwelling on things. Three hours later, I'd managed to identify eight hundred rare books to be offered at a forty percent discount to high-end dealers. It represented a fourth of the stock given to Riverrun by Pillow Wilkes and a major portion of my soul to boot. I picked up the phone and started making long-distance calls with a very heavy heart.

Around four o'clock, I was still leaving messages when I heard a rattling at the front door. Josie, who had been sitting at the counter, jumped to her feet and rushed to open it. I peered out of my office to see her usher in a handsome man in a motorized wheelchair.

He was in his mid-thirties with thick blond hair, a boyish upturned nose, and a wide, sensual mouth that, while it looked amicable enough for the moment, threatened to harden at the first sign of trouble. A small enamel pin featuring an eagle atop a globe and anchor adorned the buttonhole of his coat's lapel. His shorts ended a couple of inches above the stumps where his knees and lower legs had been. His right arm ended just below the shoulder. Under a jagged pink scar, a dark-blue patch covered his right eye socket. The surviving eye was brown. It gave Josie a level stare.

"I'm looking for Mr. Bevan."

"That would be me," I said, walking over to him. "And this is my partner, Josie Majansik."

"A pleasure. My name is Dennis Dietz."

I regarded him in amazement; not only because I was meeting this ghost from Emery's troubled past, but that such a cruelly mangled person could appear so vibrant.

He clutched Josie's fingers with his left hand, then mine. The calloused grip was uncomfortably firm.

"I'd hoped to meet you in Lawrence under more pleasant circumstances," Dietz said, handing me an embossed business card that said Biomechatronic Solutions. It had a Sunnydale, California, address. "What a tragedy about the poor woman and her handyman. No sign of the *Book of Mormon*, I suppose?"

Still somewhat bewildered, I shrugged my shoulders, pulled up a chair next to him, and sat down.

"When did you get in town?" I finally asked after Josie returned to the counter.

"This morning. I read about the fire while I was waiting for my bag at the airport."

He jiggled the joystick controller at the front of the left armrest to guide closer to me, then leaned his elbow behind it to better position himself. "Mind if I ask who commissioned you to sell the book?"

"I'm not at liberty to say."

A knowing smile emerged, displaying a row of perfect porcelain teeth, testimony to Navy reconstruction dentistry.

"Miss Darp said the same thing when I phoned her."

I nodded at the pin on his coat lapel. "What outfit were you in?"

"Third Battalion, Fifth Marines."

"Darkhorse Battalion, huh? You took some heavy shit in Helmand Province."

"Yes," Dietz said. The smile became fainter. Despite his friendly tone, his lone eye had not once ceased sizing me up. "Twenty-five dead and a hundred eighty-four wounded in seven months. We handled them in the firefights, but the IEDs evened the odds."

I nodded in sympathy but said no more.

"I'm glad we had a chance to meet," he said. "Please tell my cousin I'll be at the Raphael Hotel until Wednesday."

"Mr. Dietz…"

He held up his hand. "No need to confirm or deny, Mr. Bevan. I respect client confidentiality. Just tell Em you saw me. That's if you should run across him. I hear Kansas City's a small town that way. Everybody knows everybody."

"But not everybody's business," I said to myself.

There was a muted whir as he activated the gear motor and headed for the door. I escorted him out of the shop, but once on the sidewalk, he declined further assistance, his voice betraying only slightly the resentment of a proud man too often dependent on others.

I retreated into the store. And I watched with Josie as he manipulated his way across the busy street to his van in the church parking lot. He activated the power chair hitch carrier, rolled onto the lift platform and disappeared into the back. A few minutes later, he settled behind the steering wheel and drove away, leaving us gaping in awe at his undaunted spirit.

Grandpa Malachy Bevan once told me that a dog on three legs ain't always lame. I never understood what that meant until I met Dennis Dietz.

Chapter 14

Cue the violins.

I seem to be one of those unfortunates for whom trouble comes in wheelbarrows. No matter how much I try to prepare for turbulence, I always seem to find I've badly underrated the force of the winds. While my horrors haven't been the major league back-streets-of-Calcutta kind of daily misery—or the hell First Lieutenant Dietz must have experienced—they've been nasty enough at times. After all, how many can claim to have been barbecued in a Māori hāngī oven, had his ribs tickled by a crossbow dart, or cascaded ass-over-teakettle down a freezing subterranean cataract?

Not many, I'll warrant.

Problems were piling up, and none looked to have promising solutions. It was going to be difficult to get a proper price on such short notice for my stock. That meant unloading far more than I could afford for Riverrun to remain a respectable purveyor of rare books. Having lost all hope of gaining membership in the ABAA, it probably didn't matter anyway. Not only had my chief sponsor died, but I was responsible for allowing a client's incredibly rare book to burn with her. A definite black mark on the resume.

And then there was the little matter of preventing incest between my natural offspring without explaining why to either of them.

I knew there was no way I could convince Anne without telling her the truth, so I decided to do an end run and speak to Mark. But when I called his apartment in Lawrence, his roommate informed me that he'd flown to Denver that morning. He planned to rent a car and meet Anne in Aspen at the Fasching Haus condos the next day. I hung up and desperately began logging on to the computer for flights to Colorado. Everything was booked, leaving me with two options: trust my rotten luck to standby or drive eight hundred miles.

Given my history, guess what I chose.

Fourteen road-weary hours on I-70 later, I pulled into Aspen just as the morning sun was kissing the top of the peaks. I found the condo nestled at the base of Aspen Mountain and parked my Jeep next to a rental Nissan. It had to be Mark's because there was a KU baseball cap on the dashboard. After getting Anne's room number from the concierge—it took showing my driver's license and a picture taken of her when she was sixteen that, for some reason, I still kept in my wallet—I rushed up three flights of stairs to number 312.

I knocked on the door with my heart shaking like a trip-hammer—the combined effect of oxygen depriva-tion at ten thousand feet, eight hundred nonstop miles in a car, and an overloaded nervous system. There was the sound of scuffling of feet, and a few seconds later, my daughter opened the door wearing bulky flannel pajamas. She had never looked more innocent or adorable.

"Dad! Oh my god! It's great to see you, but what are you doing here?"

"I needed to see you in person. There's something…"

"Who is it, Anne?"

It was Mark's voice, and it came from the bedroom. He soon appeared by her side wearing a faded Jayhawk T-shirt and a pair of khaki hiking shorts. If he was bothered to see me, he had the good manners not to show it. Another fine quality of the lad's.

"Howdy, Mr. Bevan. You here to climb with us?"

I opened my mouth once or twice, but no words came out. Seeing them standing next to each other, I couldn't believe I hadn't made the connection before. It wasn't only that they were stunningly attractive. Each had my bearing, wide shoulders, and slight cleft in the chin, and while Anne's beauty came from Carol and Mark's dreamy eyes from Alice, they both had the indelible Bevan stamp. I wouldn't call it style, more like an inclination toward orneriness that, while sometimes irritating, was never boring. The latter was less pronounced in Mark, but given time, he'd rival Anne and me in the mischief-making business.

There was no point in lying or beating around the bush with these two. Alice might never speak to me again, but there was simply no alternative if I wished to avoid contributing to a Class C felony. Anyway, what's the point of sharing a secret if you can't betray it when it suits you?

"I'm not here to hike," I said, failing in my effort to avoid sounding melodramatic. "Annie. Mark. There's something you need to know."

"Really?" my daughter said with the tiniest smile as she draped an arm over Mark's shoulder.

"Uh, I wouldn't do that, honey," I said.

"Why on earth not?" she asked as she kissed him on the cheek.

"Ah, Jeeesuss," I muttered, sweating like a pack-horse. "Because you…and…he…are…"

"Half brother and sister!" they answered gleefully in unison.

You could have slapped me with a wet dolphin and I'd ask for another. Adding to my mystification, the young degenerates had the audacity to giggle at my discomfiture.

"Look, you two," I sputtered. "I'm no bluenose, but the last time I checked, cavorting under the sheets with one's sibling isn't condoned in this country—some mountain hollows in southern Missouri notwithstanding."

Before I could climb higher on my high horse, however, Annie stopped laughing long enough to tell me to relax.

"Relax? How can I do that when—"

"Mark and I figured this out a year ago when I was in rehab. There were so many mannerisms we had in common, so many things we felt the same way about. We also knew how close you and Alice were at one time. I ordered a 23andMe DNA kit to confirm it. Only cost ninety-nine bucks."

Mark slipped away from under Anne's arm and took my hand.

"Don't worry, Mr. Bevan—er—Dad. We know

how sensitive this is for everyone, especially my mom. Every time Anne and I have gotten together, it was to make up for lost time. It's been wonderful."

"So no hanky-panky?" I managed.

"Oh, Father," Anne squealed. "Don't be gross. Yuck!"

"Whew," I said.

"There's something else, though," Mark said. "My other dad is aware of the situation. He sensed something after I'd received the DNA results and confronted me with questions. I had no choice but to answer truthfully."

"How did he take it?"

"Really well, maybe because he'd suspected for a long time—even before I was born. He raised me despite that and kept the secret. He can be strict and demanding, but he's been a wonderful father to me, and Mother, in her own way, loves him deeply. Perhaps you and he should talk about it?"

Ah, from the mouth of babes.

It certainly explained a few things. Over the years, Tim Winter had kept me on at our law firm a lot longer than he needed to when I was overwhelmed by personal problems. After I was disbarred, he even loaned me start-up money for Riverrun. All of that was probably due to Alice's influence, which must have added to his already smoldering resentment toward me.

"That leaves your mom as the odd person out," I told my offspring. "I promised her I'd not tell either one of you. It's very important to her sense of self-esteem that she believes you don't know."

Mark looked at Anne then back to me.

"I think Dad would prefer to keep her in the dark as well. That's if you're okay with that."

"But she'll always insist on keeping you two apart."

"I don't think that will be a problem, Mr. Bevan."

The voice belonged to a statuesque woman just on the other side of thirty who emerged from the kitchen. Her high cheekbones and long legs in tailored trousers reminded me instantly of Katharine Hepburn after an afternoon on the golf course. More handsome than classically beautiful, this woman had that masterful air that first-rate artists or successful entrepreneurs always seem to have.

"I'm Lois Tamblyn," she said, sliding past Mark and Anne to grasp me by the arm. "I've been dying to meet you."

"My pleasure," I said, thinking that Mark had done very nicely for himself. "Is this your condo?"

"Yes. My main house is in Los Gatos, but this is convenient whenever I wish to be with Anne."

"Lois owns vineyards in the Santa Cruz Mountains," Anne added proudly while clasping the woman's hand.

"What do you mean 'convenient'?" I asked.

After a moment's bewilderment, followed by a lightning bolt of realization, I stood there like a marionette without a handler, an inane grin stitched on my face. Lois Tamblyn wasn't Mark's Mrs. Robinson. She was my daughter's.

"Just look at it this way, Pops," my new son said. "Now you can tell my mom she doesn't have to worry about Anne and me."

That afternoon, while my young'uns climbed the Maroon Bells, Lois and I spent the afternoon at the Woody Creek Tavern getting to know each other over a pitcher of margaritas. The lady was something else —Stanford grad, self-made millionaire, owner of a highly rated Northern California winery, and funny as hell. That night the kids joined us for steak and baked potatoes at the condo. As we sat at the table to eat, I raised a glass of wine to propose a toast. But due to my swelling emotions, augmented by the earlier tequila lubrication at Woody Creek, my gift of gab had deserted me. There was nothing for it, but to fall back on a rugby chant as inelegant as it was meaningless:

"Cheers, big ears! And here's to the ladies what love 'em!"

Lois, Annie, and Mark drank to it anyway. After all, we were family.

Early the next morning, I headed back to Kansas City knowing that my daughter, perhaps for the first time in her life, felt complete and truly happy.

And that, despite the loss of Stagg's *Book of Mormon* and the uncertain future of Riverrun Books, made everything seem almost right again.

Chapter 15

W*hat's she got those people rehearsing for? Some kind of crazy Irish play about a Jew walking around his town. He plays with himself, pisses in an alley, and gets walloped by a whore. Disgusting. Hope she don't let her kid see it. I want my intended pure when the time comes.*

━━━

THE SATURDAY after my return from the Rocky Mountains, the drizzle had turned into a downpour when the last frenzied attack began. I held my ground before the thundering onslaught of rampaging muscle and bone as the oblong thing above the turf began its descent. Craning my neck to focus on the spiraling gray blur among the raindrops, I sprinted two meters, then leaped high into the air, turning slightly to present my back to the charge. The jump was timed perfectly, enabling me to catch the rain-slickened rubber over my shoulder just as the first three behemoths smashed into my spine and upper legs.

I landed on my feet an instant before the next wave crashed into my battered torso. Digging my heels in the mud, I desperately fought off the flailing hands trying to rip away the ball long enough for Joe Tuitama and Buck Martin to bind onto me.

Now that I had support, I dropped to the turf and did a controlled release of the ball while still protecting it in the comma-like fold of my prone body. A ruck immediately formed over me. More pushing and clawing followed until our scrum-half whisked the ball to the stand-off who crashed ahead for fifteen meters before succumbing to a barrage of tackles.

No matter. The mêlée ended a second later with the blowing of the referee's whistle. With my defensive catch five meters from the St. Louis Bombers' try line, we had won by the narrowest of margins, showing yet again that that old age and treachery invariably trump youth and inexperience.

I staggered to my feet, a little worse for wear from a cleat to the forehead. Limping like Quasimodo to my Jeep, I felt no pain knowing that I'd secured a place on the team going to Aspen.

Ahem. How I do go on.

As Josie can tell you, listeners' eyes dart away like moths at twilight when I start describing aspects of the pastime that I hold as dear to my heart as the book trade. But this modest digression has allowed me to introduce Leau "Joe" Tuitama, the Kansas City Blues' 260-pound Samoan prop who also happened to be a devout Latter-day Saint. I figured he might answer a few questions niggling in my brain.

The rugby team was hosting the St. Louis Bombers

at The Peanut that night. Before the usual asinine revelry began, I collared Joe at a corner table where he sat Buddha-like in front of a huge overflowing plate of buffalo wings.

"You gonna eat all those?" I asked, sidling in the chair across from him.

He looked up from the plate, his olive-pit eyes suggesting I might have been a tad presumptuous.

I took a different tact.

"Buy you a drink?"

He nodded his enormous head.

I caught Pegeen Flynn's eye and held up two fingers, it being unnecessary to tell the world's greatest barmaid what her regulars wanted.

By the time she brought my Cuba libre and Joe's sixteen-liter Diet Sprite, I'd snatched half a dozen of the wings. Between delicate chomps on the tiny chicken bones, I mentioned my encounter with a couple of Joe's fellow Mormons.

"So?"

"Do you know Emery Stagg?"

"Heard of him, but he's not in my ward."

"He owned an important edition of the *Book of Mormon*."

"Good for him."

I reached for another wing. His left paw said otherwise.

"Mind if I ask what brought you to Missouri?"

"An airplane."

Like most of his clan, Joe Tuitama was a jokester.

"No, really. Why have so many Islanders settled in Jackson County?"

He looked at me as if I'd asked for money.

Finally, he said, "It's where Jesus will return."

"Says who?"

"The Prophet Joseph Smith, Jr. My folks came from Samoa when I was a kid to prepare for the Coming. My dad and uncles helped build the Temple."

"I still don't understand. Why would Pacific Islanders join a faith that—for the first hundred and fifty years anyway—was basically a white person's religion?"

"We're as Mormon as anyone," Joe answered. "We come from an explorer named Hagoth, a Nephite whose people left Israel for the Western Sea."

Was he speaking symbolically or, unlike Emery, did he really believe this moonshine? A rugby post-party in a Kansas City dive bar wasn't the place for religious debate, but I couldn't resist challenging him.

"But Smith claimed the Nephites were white. I thought the ancestors of brown-skinned Saints were called the Laminites."

He shrugged. "That's the Indians. They're descended from Lehi who left Jerusalem for America six hundred years before Christ."

"Indians? Like the Sioux?"

Joe swiped his face with a napkin already brimming with vinegar sauce. "Sure. Comanches and Apache and all of them as well, I guess. Some say we're from the Laminites, too. We're all sons of Abraham, though, ain't we?"

It was a point that could have been made by any Christian, Muslim, or Jew.

"Yeah, Joe. Amen to that."

I let the topic drop and ordered another rum from Pegeen.

About then, a few of the Bombers challenged the Blues to match them in rugby songs. The onset of obscene lyrics was Joe's cue to go home to his wife and five kids. Before leaving, however, he placed a massive hand on my shoulder and said, "Just so you know, Mike. There's a man come to town askin' about this Emery fella. Calls himself a Saint, but my ta'ma"—father—"says he has the look of a Destroying Angel. You watch your back."

Joe was gone before I could get specifics, but by then, I'd noticed someone else peripherally connected to Stagg's book.

Buford Higgins sat at the end of the bar looking more than a little disgruntled at the antics of the mud-bedecked hooligans who had invaded his favorite watering hole. I wrapped the last of the chicken wings in a napkin and made my way past the choristers who had just begun to belt out "Charlotte the Harlot" at the top of their leathery lungs.

"Aren't you a little old to be playing in the mud?" Buford shouted as I bellied up to the bar next to him.

"'Tho' much is taken, much abides,'" I intoned, "'and tho' we are not now that strength which in old days moved earth and heaven, that which we are, we are…'"

He looked at me quizzically until a light went on under his hat and he responded in kind. "'One equal temper of heroic hearts, made weak by time and fate, but strong in will…'"

I joined with him on the last line, "'To strive, to seek, to find, and not to yield.'"

The lines we'd recited were from Alfred Lord Tennyson's *Ulysses*, which Josie had read at Buford's retirement party from the police force. I knew that ever since then he'd carried the poem in his wallet, but I was surprised to find he'd actually memorized it.

Not for the first time did I realize there was more to the crusty former cop than I'd given credit.

"I saw you on the news the other day," I mentioned after we had clinked glasses.

"The Lawrence fire?"

"Yeah. What were you doing up there?"

"I'd been at the university's pathology lab that afternoon. Dropped by to offer help when I heard the sirens." He drained his beer. "What a cock-up that investigation was."

"What do you mean?"

"The male didn't die as a result of the fire. While I was helping to body-bag him, I noticed a small round indentation at the back of his skull. I mentioned this to the Douglas County coroner, but he brushed it off at first, claiming the cause of death was from burns. He insisted the head injury was a result of failing lumber or some such shit. Finally, one of his assistants checked the lungs."

"And there was no evidence of smoke inhalation," I volunteered uneasily.

"Bingo. The man had to have been killed by a blow to the head before the fire reached him."

"Damn. That sure puts a different light on things. What about Miss Darp?"

"Smoke probably killed her while she slept, then the flames. Not pretty, in either case. The police aren't getting the word out until they've finished the on-site investigation…hey, you look a little green. Are you okay?"

No. Not by a long shot, and this time, it wasn't my bowels. I should have finished my drink, paid the bill, and after telling Buford I'd be in touch, headed for home.

Instead I smiled and emptied my glass.

Perhaps one day I'll learn that temperance is a bridle of gold, passion's bride, and the strength of the soul. But this unwelcome news had scared the bejesus out of me, and alcohol seemed a more reasonable antidote to my fear than pulling bedcovers over my head next to Josie.

So I ordered another round after Buford left and joined my rugby mates in a rousing rendition of "Zulu Warrior." When following that, the Blues' captain declared me Man of the Match, I was happy enough to be twins and only too ready to acknowledge the honor by the traditional chugging of ale from an old boot. The effort magically erased, for a few hours at least, all the problems in the universe.

Two hours later, I handed the keys to my Jeep to the bartender for safekeeping and walked home as legless as a cow on roller skates.

Victor Ludorum—champion athlete—indeed.

Chapter 16

Emery and I sat in Café Provence's front room at nine o'clock the next morning. My body ached from the bashing on the rugby pitch the day before, but not as badly as my head from the post-game festivities. It wasn't the first time I'd asked myself why the hell I played the game. Two hours earlier, still stinking of liniment and stale beer, I'd taken a good long look in the mirror.

It wasn't the nose that had taken a sideways detour or the damaged cartilage in the right ear, making it resemble a squashed potato that concerned me. I'd become accustomed to the battle scars a long time ago, and as Josie liked to say, they added character to a face that would otherwise have been a little too winsome. Rather, it was the realization that I might be two or three head knocks from becoming a case study for early dementia.

Between cautious sips of hot chocolate, I struggled to focus on what Emery had to say regarding the meeting he'd had with Denny Dietz while I was whooping it up at The Peanut. Apparently, he and his cousin had gotten along like cream cheese and a bagel. I decided not to tell him, for the moment at least, that the fire in Lawrence had become a homicide investigation.

"I should have offered the book to him first," Emery said, still smarting over the way I'd lost his treasure.

"So why didn't you?"

"I had no idea Denny had the kind of money you said the book would be worth. But I also wanted to keep my distance from him because of our pact."

"I thought you said his father was a rich car dealer."

"He was when Denny was growing up. But the old man lost his shirt after trading his Toyota dealerships for Hummer franchises and died from a heart attack when Dennis was in college."

"But Eula Darp said book dealers out west vouched for his ability to pay?"

"My cousin always had grit to go with his brains," Emery answered. "He not only survived emotionally from his horrific injuries, but he invested a small inheritance from his father to start a venture capital firm in Silicon Valley. Made a bundle."

"Why was he so interested in getting your *Book of Mormon*?"

"He wanted to keep an important piece of Stagg history in family hands. But that wasn't all of it. He saw it as an opportunity to reconnect with me."

"To question why you hadn't complied with your oath?"

"That's what I feared. But when we met yesterday, his first words were that blood atonement was contrary to all that the LDS Church represents. He realized it the day he awoke in the triage unit on the outskirts of Musa Qal'ah."

"You're sure he was sincere?"

"You don't go through what Denny experienced and not have a different, clearer perspective on things."

"If that was the case, why didn't he contact you before?"

"He didn't know how to get in touch with me until he noticed the Stagg *Book of Mormon* had come on the market in Kansas. He'd also planned to warn Natalie, but he lost track of her when she moved from Boston. Finally, he believed that as long as he, Denny, remained alive, Uncle Lamar would not demand that the cudgel be passed to me."

"Sounds pretty naïve for a successful businessman."

"Perhaps. But Lamar thought a great deal of him. Looking back on it, I think far more than he did of me and Porter. It wasn't until our uncle informed him personally that he realized I'd become the chosen avenger."

"So the matter is resolved."

"Hardly."

"I thought you might say that," I said grimly. "The fire in Lawrence was no accident. It's been reclassified as arson and double homicide."

Emery caught his breath, then said, "Toward the end of our conversation, Denny asked—almost in passing—if I was aware Porter Grint had been released from prison."

"When?"

"Two weeks ago. Six months before that, a barmaid linking Porter to the murder recanted her testimony, claiming he'd acted in self-defense. The case had been set for a retrial when it looked like she'd changed her mind again, but then her corpse showed up in a shallow grave. The prosecutor had no choice but to drop charges."

"So Porter still has friends who think like he does?"

"It would appear so. And they obviously got to that barmaid."

I told him what Joe Tuitama had said.

"It's got to be Porter looking for me," Emery said. "I'm taking Natalie and Claire away from here."

"That's no good," I said. "He'll find you eventually. You must go to the police with this. If you don't call them today, I will."

He didn't see it that way.

"We're leaving. I'm going to need that money you promised right away."

"But I've told you, it will take at least three months to sell enough of my stock to pay you."

Emery gave me a level stare and said, almost apologetically, "I suggest then that you take out a loan from your favorite banker. Given Riverrun's impressive inventory, I'm sure Edward Worth would grant your request."

He was using the same words I'd given to Natalie for raising funds at the Celtic Center.

I answered with a sour grin. Paying the bill, I made a mental note: If any of us survived the wrath of blood atonement, I'd cut Emery and Natalie's wedding gift by half.

Chapter 17

Back in the shop, I glumly explained to Josie what had transpired.

"Excuse me," she said. "A convicted murderer who intends to kill Natalie is on the loose? And you're worried about having to get a loan?"

"It's not the loan itself so much as the new time frame. Anyway, they shouldn't be thinking of leaving. The guy will find them wherever they go. Better to be among friends."

"Okay, I totally agree with that last part," Josie said, "but you still need to come up with the dough. Might as well get it over with right now."

"What d'ya mean 'right now'?"

Josie tilted her head toward the sidewalk where a handsome couple strolled hand in hand toward the bistro.

Bloody hell, as my daughter would say. It was none other than Edward Stuyvesant Worth IV and Sandra Epstein exchanging goo-goo eyes at each other. It wasn't enough that Eddie was richer than Croesus or that his bank held the note to my store; he had nearly stolen Josie from me two years earlier and now he was going after my favorite second-chair symphony flutist.

It was churlishly absurd of me to feel jealous, seeing as how I was engaged to Ms. Wonderful, but I couldn't help the rush of blood to my cheeks when I saw them so obviously enamored of each other. Sandra and I had never consummated our relationship, but that's only because she had somebody when I didn't and vice versa. She was cute as a button with pouty lips, dimpled cheeks, silky black hair, and Liz Taylor eyes. And while her body didn't match Majansik's (outside a certain trapeze artist with Cirque du Soleil, whose does?), had circumstances been otherwise, I wouldn't have kicked her out of bed for eating crackers.

But I'm glad I never got the chance.

We were pals, you see, Sandra and I, mutual admirers who laughed at each other's jokes and loved to perform together during impromptu Friday night sessions at Fitzpatrick's Galway Pub, she on the tin whistle and me with my tonsils, which, as I may have modestly said somewhere before, can make the angels gnaw their wingtips with envy. Why ruin all that with carnal knowledge?

I was halfway through a fit of coughing when I noticed that my fiancée had the same high color on her face. And she hadn't even bothered to hide it.

"Hey," I said indignantly. "You still have the hots for him."

"Oh, and your tongue wasn't hanging out when you saw Sandra?"

"Wanna see if they'll swap?" I teased.

"You are disgusting, Bevan." Then, as if reconsidering, she added, "Okay, yeah. But I don't think they'll go for it."

"You sure?"

Josie studied me for a second, like the proverbial bird eyeing a worm.

"I hate to dash your fantasies, Michael, but I really am joking. Are you?"

I pretended to ponder the question—helps to keep 'em off-balance, you know—before pledging my eternal fidelity.

"In that case, lover boy, I suggest you ask Eddie right now to add a few more zeros to what we already owe his bank."

"All right, but I'm not going in there alone. You come with me to help me avoid temptation."

Worth and Epstein—under the circumstances it helped to think of them objectively by their surnames —had settled in a far corner of the bistro, sitting next to each other with their backs against the wall, eyes only for each other. Josie and I trudged toward them feeling like Russian serfs come to seek impossible concessions from the village commissar.

It took a few moments standing in front of their table before Worth arched his sleek head in my direction. I could smell the Eucris pomade in his slicked-back hair. That was Eddy all right: a real dandy, cut from the same Eastern prep-school cloth of his forebears. He was a good-looking man, a decade or so younger than me. Tall, fit, and an immaculate dresser who traveled to London's Jermyn Street each year to be fitted for his ten-thousand-dollar bespoke suits. Even women who were unaware of his immense family wealth and Mayflower pedigree were attracted to him.

I gave him points for courage as well, having watched his unflappable performance assisting Josie when she worked undercover for the FBI. I would have liked him better if he hadn't asked her to marry him after it. At least he hadn't hit on Pegeen Flynn. I'm not so sure about Alice Winter, however.

"Hiya, Ed."

"Hello, Mike." He turned to Josie with a smile altogether too big. "And it's great to see you, Josephine."

Sandra saw their eye contact and didn't like it. She glided her gun turrets at me. Her lips remained tightly shut, but "*Why are you interrupting us?*" seeped from her pores.

"Will you be in the office tomorrow?" I asked the banker.

"Why? You need more money?"

"A hundred fifty thousand. Perhaps more in three months."

"No way, Bevan. I may be a coldhearted financier, but I don't want to be the one who pulls the plug on Riverrun when you can't repay. The community would never forgive me."

"My house is paid for."

His look softened. "You'd mortgage that?"

"For this, I would."

Worth looked at Josie. She nodded.

"All right. Come by at nine-thirty tomorrow. I've no problem kicking you out of your home, if need be."

"Thank you, Eddie," Josie responded. "What a sweetheart you are."

Ms. Epstein emitted the slightest "harrumph."

"Sandra," I said, hoping to relieve the tension. "Have you played any gigs at Fitzpatrick's lately?"

She rubbed her throat provocatively and said,

"Yeah, but I haven't performed 'The Wind that Shakes the Barley' for months. Maybe we can get together for old times' sake. We were good together, weren't we? Music wise, that is."

This time it was Josie's turn to harrumph while surreptitiously pinching me on the butt.

Nary a word was exchanged when we returned to the store. Eye contact remained nil while we settled into a domestic implosion that had as much to do with exhaustion from stress as anything else.

Affection is a lot like melancholy, in which trifles can sometimes get magnified. Our sarcastic jousting had suddenly become way too serious in our desperate attempt to forget our troubles, financial and otherwise. But more than that, I'd forgotten how insecure Josie could be when it came to our relationship.

Later, at home, even our demon cat sensed the frigidity. But instead of keeping his distance from either of us, Feklar made it a point to circle one then the other's legs, accompanied by a piteous meowing even after he'd gone through two cans of tuna.

It was enough to break Bluebeard's heart. I muttered some inanities to Josie from time to time, hoping to rekindle that ineffable spark in our relationship, but my attempts were met with impassive silence. Around ten, she headed up the stairs with the cat hanging over her shoulder. I tentatively followed, keeping a cautionary four steps behind.

The blood of Attila did not course through Ms. Majansik for nothing. She could be as cruel as any rampaging Hun when it came to making my nervous system approach meltdown with the thought of losing her.

And yet…

In the bedroom, I watched from the door as she set Feklar on a chair and began to shed her clothes unhurriedly. When she was down to her underwear, she turned to face me. She had a gymnast's body, about middle height, slender but muscular, with firm breasts, a tiny waist, and sinewy thighs that looked as if they could crush walnuts. But it was the look of forgiveness on that beautiful, gamine face that made me realize what she truly meant to me.

"Before we get some sleep," she said, "I thought…"

Her unfinished sentence hung in the air and I was on her like a cougar in heat, tearing off my clothes, spouting endearments and foregoing all the preliminaries Alex Comfort used to preach about. Once we hit the sheets, the pace was too hot to last long, and soon, we were languishing in each other's arms, exhausted but blissful.

It had been feverish work, but half an hour later, Josie's tickling fingers hinted at a more leisurely encore. Tuckered as I was, I set aside the paperback I'd been reading and manfully prepared to rise to the occasion.

Just as the telephone rang.

"Mike!" Natalie whispered desperately. "Thank God you're there. Emery isn't answering his phone and I think someone is in—"

She didn't finish her sentence. I heard Claire's high-pitched keen in the background before the line went dead.

Chapter 18

S *ays he woulda had the bitch if the kid's screech hadn't put him off his mark. We'll find her again. A quick double slash under the chin the way Uncle Lamar taught, usin' the sheep. Once learned, you never forget. Like riding a bicycle. Or screwing. Even after twelve years. Take the girl with me. Teach her wifely ways in Mexico. I got time. Where in the hell did they get to?*

▬▬

THERE WERE two police cars on the street in front and another in the alley behind the house when we pulled up. Natalie and Claire had just returned, escorted by a female officer. They had fled in their pajamas to the PayDay Loan Center a block away. Both of them perked up upon seeing us and after assuring the police that we were the ones who had dialed 911, we were allowed inside.

It was nearing the end of the officers' evening shift —the hazard-pay hours—and the sergeant seemed impatient to get our statements. He looked familiar. I realized I'd seen him in Café Provence's kitchen chatting up the cook and getting free croissants.

A pair of officers proceeded to the screened-in porch to dust for fingerprints and I went into the tiny kitchen to make a pot of coffee. Josie took a seat next to Claire at the dining room table. After changing into jeans and a sweatshirt, Natalie returned to the living room, where she sat on the couch.

"I'm Sergeant Turvey, ma'am. Did you or your daughter get a good look at the intruder?"

Natalie shook her head. "We were out the door as soon as we heard the window break in the bedroom… Sergeant, I'm really worried about my fiancé. Couldn't you send a car to check on him? He lives in the Twain Apartments, 2445 Jefferson, just west of the Plaza."

Turvey dutifully placed a call to headquarters relaying the request and address; then, with a glance at his watch, the sergeant resumed his questioning.

While Natalie detailed what she knew concerning Emery and his cousins' pact with blood atonement to an increasingly confused policeman, I waited for the coffee to percolate and eavesdropped on the officers who were dusting for fingerprints in the back bedroom.

"I hate these prowler runs," the younger of the two complained. "The creeps are always long gone by the time we show up."

"What d'ya expect, rookie?" the woman cop said. "Gotta let the customers think we're on top of things. Get used to it."

Forty minutes later, Josie and I finished providing our statements. The sergeant's face indicated that he hadn't understood or believed a word of what we had said, but he promised to have a patrol watch the house for the next few days.

Natalie looked skeptical. "You mean they'll cruise the neighborhood once in the morning and once at night?"

"It's more than that, ma'am. We vary the schedule. I promise you'll be protected."

This time it was Josie who spoke up. "You did hear us say for the past hour that this Porter Grint is a convicted murderer? One who has expressed his intent to kill Ms. Phelan?"

"I got it all, miss. But I'm not going to issue an all-points bulletin for a man whose conviction was over-thrown and who was legally released from prison—not unless we get some prints showing he was here."

He looked over at me. "Your bookstore's not far from here, Bevan. You must know we get half a dozen reports of home intrusions every week. Dollars to doughnuts this was a local kid who won't come back now that he knows we're watching."

"Be that as it may," I said, "We'll stay here tonight."

"Suit yourself, but I don't think it's necessary."

With that, Josie shot him a look that said she didn't give a rat's ass what he thought.

After the police had gone, Natalie tucked Claire in her bed and returned to the living room, cell phone in hand.

"He's still not answering," she told us.

Chapter 19

That'll teach him to defy Lamar. Just took cutting the tie rod, and the Buick flew through that railing like it wasn't there. Shoulda finished the job with a Ka-bar but couldn't with them two Samaritans clamberin' down the ridge to help. Likely ol' Em's a goner anyway.

◼

AROUND MIDNIGHT, a subdued and considerably more contrite Sergeant Turvey returned with the news that Emery's car had gone off an embankment on Sixty-third Street near Swope Park. He wasn't dead, but he was in serious condition with a fractured skull and internal injuries.

Once Natalie got her emotions under control, Turvey said a detective would be contacting her and us for more details about the "Mormon thing."

Josie cradled Claire Phelan in her arms as we waited in the visitors' area outside the Intensive Care Unit of St. Luke's Hospital.

Natalie emerged from the ICU after an hour.

"He's in a coma," she said. "They're very concerned about swelling of the brain. I…I think we might lose him."

Instinctively, I looked at Claire, who continued to rock in Josie's arms. Her eyes stared at the ceiling tiles and her lips were pulled back with her upper teeth clenching her lower lip, but she remained silent.

"Do you want us to contact his parents?" Josie asked Natalie.

"I already have," she answered. "They'll be here tomorrow."

"No need for you two to return to your house," I said. "You can stay with us until they catch that guy."

"Thank you. Take Claire with you, but I want to stay near the hospital for the next few days."

"Are you sure?"

"Yes. The police were kind enough to check me in under a pseudonym at the Express Holiday Inn across the street."

She took her house keys out of her purse and gave them to Josie. "Do you mind picking up some clothes and personals for us?"

"Right," Josie said. "I'll get them right away."

I got a call to report to the Central Patrol Division Station to talk to a Detective Fletcher. He didn't fit the profile of a big-city cop. For one thing, he was really skinny. Barney Fife skinny. A hundred thirty pounds soaking wet. For another, he lisped. But not like a girl. Like Lou Holtz, the former Notre Dame football coach, his mouth produced excess saliva when he spoke. Sometimes he was able to avoid "sh" and sometimes not.

Fletcher met me in the foyer. First thing out of his

mouth was how "pished" he was the way Buford Higgins had been treated. Then he invited me into his cubbyhole of an office.

"I read Turvey's report," he said as he settled behind his desk. "It gets pretty garbled when he tries to describe what you shaid happened in Lawrence. But the Douglas County Sheriff confirmed that thanks to Higgins, they're treating the fire and subsequent deaths as a homicide investigation."

I repeated what I knew about Eulalia Darp and Norman Tate, how their deaths were in all likelihood linked to an inscribed *Book of Mormon*, and that I'd tried to broker its sale for Emery Stagg.

"You alsho say that Emery's other cousin, thish—this—Dietz fellow, had traveled all the way from California to Kansas to look at it on the day of the fire?"

"That's right."

"Then why shouldn't we be worried about him, considering that he was in on this shupposed blood atonement pact at one time?"

"I can think of one very good reason. There's nothing wrong with him that a miracle couldn't fix, but perhaps you'd like to speak to him yourself."

"Give him a call."

I pulled out Dennis Dietz's business card and dialed his cell phone number.

He sounded groggy when he answered, a surprise since it was only eleven p.m. in California.

"Denny, this is Mike Bevan. Your cousin's been in a car accident."

"Cousin? Which…you mean Emery?"

"Yeah. He's in critical condition. Skull fracture, among other things. Someone tampered with his car."

"What are his chances?" he asked, his voice turning somber.

"He's clinging to life. Barely."

"Sheez."

"The police have asked if he had any enemies."

"What did you tell them?"

"Everything I know about the pact to kill Natalie. I'm sitting here with Detective Fletcher of the Kansas City Police Department. He'd like to speak to you."

Five seconds of silence.

"You were right to do so, of course, Bevan. Put me on the speakerphone."

After waiving his right to self-incrimination, Dennis agreed to Fletcher's recording the conversation and over the next half hour, corroborated everything Emery had told me.

"So, Mr. Dietz," the detective summarized. "You're tellin' me that you were involved in shum kind of cult?"

"I'm a Mormon, sir," Dennis answered. "As well as a Marine Corps veteran. The Church of Latter-day Saints is no more a cult than Catholicism. The fanatical group I became associated with as a boy, however, chose to misinterpret something our Mormon Moses was believed to advocate."

"Mormon Moshes?"

"Brigham Young, our second prophet after Joseph Smith, Jr. Blood atonement was long ago declared an immoral tenet by succeeding presidents of the Church. I no more adhere to it than Emery Stagg, but it appears that our other cousin, Porter Grint, still does. Furthermore, as his previous manslaughter conviction attests, Porter's fully capable of murdering Mrs. Phelan."

"Have you had contact with Grint shince his release from prison?"

"No. That would've spelled more trouble than I could handle if things got hot between us."

"Oh, and why ish that?" he asked with the slightest hint of sarcasm. "You bein' a marine and all."

"Just call it circumstances beyond my control, sir. I'll leave it to Mr. Bevan to explain."

"All right, Dietz. Once I get this statement of yours typed up, I'll fax it to you for your review. I'd appreciate your shigning it and getting it back to me within forty-eight hours."

"Go ahead and send it, but I may arrive in Kansas City before then to sign it in person. When I get there, I'll answer whatever other questions you may have."

After the phone call, I told Fletcher about Dietz's disabilities.

The detective was silent for a moment.

"I knew a guy like that," he said.

"Come again?"

"Clint Carter. Legs were crushed when his patrol car flipped in a chase. Double amputee above the knees. He'd spent nearly a year in rehab, trying all sorts of things to maintain mobility without constantly relying on a wheelchair. He tried walking on fourteen-inch-high prosthetics with training feet—'shorties' they call 'em. Humiliating, but shtabilizing when you're learning to maintain balance and get to places the wheelchair won't go. It's easier on the heart rate, too."

Fletcher stopped for a long minute. I thought he had finished, and I started to get up until I realized this tough cop with twenty hard years on the force had choked up. It was past midnight, and he was officially off duty, but he wanted to talk.

"The shorties combined with the wheelchair were a good compromise for him. He wheeled competitively in half marathons and even learned to shnow ski. But Frank had too much pride. I know shumpthing about what constant embarrassment can do to you."

"What's he doing now?"

"Not a hell of a lot. Shot himself with his Glock."

"Jesus, why?"

"He liked to swim at the Police Academy pool when no one was there, using his short prosthetics to get to the edge of the pool and slide in. One day a class of recruits arrived earlier than usual for training. One wiseassh whispers to his buddies that Clint reminded him of Inspector Clousheau disguised as Touloushe Lautrec. Even if he didn't hear what was said, Clint knew what they were laughing at.

"I thought he was made of sterner stuff, but, unlike the wounded in military hospitals, he didn't have any peer support. He gave up after that."

I thought Fletcher was going to get sticky on me again, so I asked what he intended to do about Porter Grint.

His answer was to pick up the telephone and issue an APB throughout the metropolitan area, including Johnson and Wyandotte Counties in Kansas, for the ex-con's apprehension.

Dennis Dietz arrived the following morning. He went over his statement with the detective, adding more details as to how the three cousins had been brainwashed. He tried to visit Emery the next day in the ICU, but no visitors other than Natalie were allowed.

Afterward, Josie and I treated him to lunch at Café Provence. The place was crowded, but I had reserved a table. Heads turned as we came in, then abruptly turned away, as people do when encountering someone so disabled. Our server was overly solicitous as she poured our coffees, speaking painfully slowly and with careful enunciation.

After we had ordered soup and sandwiches, Josie tried to make light of the waitress's discomfort, saying the poor girl must have thought we were deaf.

"Actually," Dietz said. "I can't hear out of my right ear. That whole side of me is pretty worthless."

That threatened to put a damper on the conversation until Josie and I, feeling compelled to practically shout our sentences, suddenly got the giggles as we realized the entire place was listening in. Thankfully, Dietz saw the humor in that as well, and we returned to more normal voices once the food arrived.

It was obvious that Dennis was worried about Emery's condition, but between slurps of vichyssoise, he mentioned how sad it was that Porter clung to such a misguided belief.

"He never really had much of a chance in life," he said. "Porter worshipped Lamar and Regina, even when they punished him for breaking the rules. They were the only people who ever showed any affection for him."

"Porter killed a man," I reminded him.

"In self-defense," Dennis quickly rebutted. "He used the knife only after the bikers ganged up on him. His public defender was incompetent."

"Apparently he had a better one second time around," I said.

"The barmaid recanted her testimony."

"Don't you think she might have been coerced?" Josie asked.

"I don't know who would have done it or why. It doesn't matter anyway, now that she's dead."

Josie nearly spit out her coffee. She put down her cup. "That's a callous thing to say, don't you think?"

Dennis placed his hand on hers.

"I'm sorry, Josie. I tend to clutch at any straw when defending the indefensible deeds of my family. As Emery can tell you, it's been a terrible burden. Please forgive me."

She nodded and then lifted her hand from his grasp to resume eating her croque-monsieur sandwich.

After the waitress refilled our coffee cups, the conversation got around to our Marine Corps experiences. I had nothing to compare to his, of course. I'd been a judge advocate who rarely got away from the relative safety of battalion headquarters. Nonetheless, I'd seen action, and even had the good luck to walk away from a helicopter crash. Despite the seriousness of his wounds, a Purple Heart was the only medal Dietz received for the bad luck of being near an exploding mine. After Josie's coaxing, however, he admitted having been awarded a Silver Star during a previous deployment.

Then I asked, "How do you feel about the Taliban recovering much of the lost territory your unit took at such a huge personal cost?"

"No surprise there. It's been the pattern in Afghanistan throughout history, beginning with Alexander the Great. The problem with the world today is that, to paraphrase J. B. S. Haldane, too many leaders have an inordinate fondness for battles."

Dennis was silent for a moment as he contemplated his next words. In the background were the typical noises of a busy bistro over the noon hour—the clattering of dishes, waitresses cooing about dessert offerings, the laughter over inconsequential events, the clinking of water glasses.

Finally, he said, "Going through a war doesn't necessarily fit a person for the real world; nor however horrible one's experiences, does it make you any wiser. I vowed after they amputated my arm and the first leg that I'd not let the injuries destroy me. It was harder to accept a month later when they couldn't save the left leg, but I sucked it up. Except for a few dark periods, that's pretty much been the case. Recovery took the better part of a year. I wouldn't wish my injuries on anyone, but it opened opportunities for me."

"In what way?" Josie gently asked.

Before answering, he reached across the table to brush a crumb off her collar with his biomechanical hand. The gesture struck me as a bit much, but it had my fiancée cooing her appreciation. I could tell she was smitten by this handsome devil.

Even then he hesitated to respond, as if he feared his answer would sound boastful. But Josie, the little flirt, wasn't about to let him stop.

"Please, Dennis. We'd really like to know. Wouldn't we, Michael?"

"Sure," I said, "but we're interrupting his meal with all this talk. Perhaps—"

"Oh, it's no bother," he interjected. "It's just that I was far luckier than other guys in my situation and I feel somewhat guilty about it."

As I suspected, Dietz wasn't one to waste the chance to puff a bit for a beautiful female admirer who, by now, was practically salivating with admiration for the plucky war veteran.

"I had the good fortune," he continued, "to be

selected for an experimental rehab program at CalTech. A group of brilliant researchers were creating and testing bionic arms and legs that mimic the function of natural limbs. It was too late to help me, but I became a careful observer of this revolutionary biomechanical technology. I'd also had a knack for innovation, having designed my own surfboards as a kid. Guess I was a lot like Emery in that way. Based on what I'd learned at the tech lab, I designed a robotic ankle-foot prosthesis to help people suffering from drop foot. My little brother has cerebral palsy and the foot, as much as anything, really tormented him. The researchers helped me tweak my design for a prototype. They put me in contact with venture capitalists for a start-up."

He pronounced this in such an understated manner that you might have thought he was describing the opening of a hot dog stand after spraining his wrist.

"My god, that's wonderful, Dennis," Josie gushed.

"Thank you, but Biomech Solutions is still a long way from showing a profit."

"Given time, I have no doubt you'll succeed."

"Time is something I don't have in abundance, Josie."

Stifling a cough, he turned his head away from us and struggled to catch his breath.

"Sorry about that," he said once the color returned to his face. "I'm prone to getting blood clots. Sometimes one floats from what's left of my legs to lodge in a lung. Only a matter of time before one breaks away to my heart or brain."

He was matter of fact about it.

After lunch, Josie gave Dietz a hug then headed

into the store. This time he let me follow him to his van. Before rolling onto the lift, he stopped. "Thanks for being a friend to Emery and Natalie, Bevan. Do right by them. They deserve a normal life."

"I will," I promised. Then I shook his hand. "Semper Fidelis, Marine."

"And to you, Brother."

Chapter 20

That afternoon I left Claire with Josie at the bookstore and dropped by the hospital to check on Emery's progress.

Natalie wasn't there. She'd gone to a meeting with the director of the annual Bloomsday play. Scheduled for June sixteenth, this two-hour dramatization of James Joyce's novel *Ulysses* featured some of the best actors in the city and had become the major fundraiser for the Celtic Center. This was to be its twentieth anniversary; it couldn't be canceled.

A couple sat outside the doors of the ICU as *Jeopardy!* blared on a TV in a corner. There was no question that the man was Emery's father—over sixty, about six feet, and stout with the same upturned nose and close-set eyes. The left hinge of his glasses was wrapped in electrical tape. A mechanical pencil hung below a tuft of gray chest hair showing through the neck V of his polo shirt.

The woman was a few years younger than the man, and slim, with gentle eyes in a long, horselike face. She sat upright in the plastic chair with an air of calm not usually found in the confines of an intensive care waiting room.

After signing the visitors' chart, I introduced myself.

"Are you Emery's parents?"

The man got to his feet and extended a hand.

"Claude Stagg," he told me. "This is my wife, Marjorie."

Mrs. Stagg dipped her head politely.

"Are you a friend of our son?" she asked.

"In a manner of speaking," I replied. "He and Natalie Phelan are customers of my bookshop."

The gray, drab room got even drabber.

"You're the fellow who lost our family's book!" the man said sharply.

"That's one way of putting it. I intend to make it up to him."

Claude Stagg grunted and returned to his chair.

"I suppose that's what Em gets for trying to sell it," he groused to his wife. "There were plenty enough Staggs he could've let have it."

"But few enough willing to pay," she retorted brusquely. "It was Emery's to do with as he pleased."

"Lamar should have known better than to give it to the boy."

"There were lots of things Lamar should have known better about," she snapped.

I sat down in a yellow plastic chair opposite them. "Mind if I ask you a few questions?"

There was a dead pause as Mr. Stagg looked at his wife. She tilted her head in a sort of shrug, then clicked the mute button on the TV remote.

"Go ahead," he said. "The doc says Em'll be out for another hour before they try to wake him for us."

"Were you aware of what Lamar was running up at his camp in Grand Lake?"

The man's eyes narrowed. "That's an odd question coming from a book man."

"I'm trying to get to the bottom of things, Mr. Stagg. There's a person's life at stake."

"I don't understand," he said, then sighed heavily. "All we knew was that my brother was teaching Emery and the others outdoor ways. They were all getting a bit spoiled in their hometowns. Our boy came back a real good fisherman and much more confident. We were glad for that."

I paused when a nurse entered the waiting room to log in at the counter. She seemed vaguely familiar, but she disappeared down the hallway before I could get a better look. I edged my chair closer to the couple.

"There was more than hunting and fishing being taught there," I said. "Emery told me what he and his cousins had gone through during those summers. Those boys were being indoctrinated to commit a horrible act of revenge."

The Staggs seemed genuinely perplexed.

"Natalie Phelan, your son's fiancée, is the last living descendant of Governor Thomas Ford. The plan was originally for Porter Grint to kill her in order to atone for her ancestor's role in the assassination of Joseph Smith, Jr."

Marjorie Stagg slipped her blue-veined hand on to her husband's. In a half-whisper, she said to her husband, "I told you something was amiss that last year when Emery came back from Colorado! He'd gone into his shell like when he was little, except he wasn't our nice, unassuming boy anymore. I was almost afraid of him."

"I'm well aware of the blood atonement myth," Mr. Stagg said to me while patting his wife's hand, "but that's all it is—a myth. I don't say I abide by much of what Lamar does or believes, but he's not a criminal. He'd never do anything like that."

Marjorie pulled her hand away from him. "You say our son told you this?"

"Yes, ma'am. And it's been confirmed by Dennis Dietz. Porter Grint, Denny, and your son underwent a form of brainwashing at Lamar's lodge. They had been programmed to kill Natalie in order to satisfy a pact made over a century and a half ago by a group of Danites that included Alonzo Stagg."

"I find that hard to swallow," Claude Stagg insisted, but his voice faltered. "Lamar acted like he liked the lady when she and her girl came to Regina's funeral."

He edged toward me. "And Dennis agrees with this cockamamie tale?"

"Yes, sir. He's already given his statement to the police."

The older man sighed. "The Prophet proclaimed that a murderer should not be hung, but rather have his head cut off so his blood could spill on the ground for an offering to God. That was for a capital crime, however, not out of vengeance. If my brother appointed Porter to be the first to carry this out, when was it to happen?"

"Shortly after Natalie turned twenty-one. But Grint was sent to prison before he could act on it."

"Port always was a troublesome one," Marjorie said. "I used to say his limitations were limitless. He gave my sister and brother-in-law plenty of headaches growing up, but I never figured he was capable of murder."

"Be that as it may," her husband said, "he killed that man in Rock Springs. Doesn't matter that he claimed self-defense."

He turned back to me.

"I can see Port being capable of this, but not Dennis. And certainly not my son."

"Nonetheless," I insisted. "The obligation fell to Dietz until he was crippled and it was Emery's turn. He's admitted it, sir."

Mrs. Stagg hung her head. "Emery seemed lost for so long. He stopped visiting us. Quit going to temple. I never understood why he moved to the Midwest. It's not like he was happy in California, but...does he really love this Phelan woman?"

"Yes, and I can assure you that she loves him as well. Like Dennis, I believe Emery emerged from this nightmare a much stronger person."

"Then the only one to worry about," Stagg said, "is Porter Grint. Anyone know where he's got to?"

"Don't be a fool, Claude. Where else would he be, but here?"

Hearing the gentle woman declare this made it seem all the more menacing. Suddenly, we heard a series of agitated cries beyond the locked door of the ICU.

Then nothing. The silence filled the waiting room like mud.

Seconds later, we heard footsteps and the door swung open. A doctor stood there, wild-eyed and with blood on his green scrubs.

"Mr. and Mrs. Stagg," he said. "You'd better come with me."

I jumped to my feet but was helpless to do anything as pandemonium reigned beyond the closed door of the ICU. Within minutes, hospital security guards rushed in, soon followed by three local police officers who were immediately guided past the door by the desk nurse. I phoned Natalie's cell phone only to get her voice mail.

Another ten minutes passed before the nurse I'd noticed signing in earlier appeared behind the desk. Now I knew why she'd looked familiar: She was Arihi Tuitama, the daughter of my rugby friend, Joe. I went up to the counter where she was reviewing the visitors' sheet.

"Arihi, what's going on?"

She looked up, irritated by the interruption until she recognized me.

"We had an intruder," she said. "Dr. Misner was making his rounds when he found a man wearing a balaclava hovering over the patient. The doctor shouted at him and the guy slammed him to the floor and shot out the door. He headed down a staircase before anyone could get to him."

"How's the doctor?"

"He'll be fine, thank God. A few cuts and bruises but nothing else. I don't think Mr. Stagg was even aware of what happened. He's been comatose much of the time." She checked her watch. "Now, excuse me. I must get downstairs to make a report to my supervisor."

I followed her into the main corridor. "Who else signed in today?" I asked as she waited for the elevator to arrive.

"Stagg's parents and four other people besides you. We have no idea how he snuck in."

"Officially?"

"For the record, yes. I hope nobody loses their job over this, but unofficially, a janitor left the emergency exit ajar."

The elevator door opened, and she stepped in. "I hear you played a match with my dad Saturday."

"Somebody had to remind him how the game is played."

She smiled, said something about the virus of rugby and old thoroughbreds gone lame, and then the door closed.

I returned to the waiting room where a female police officer had just finished taking a statement from the receptionist. After giving my account, including a brief summary of the Porter Grint connection, I asked if the police had an identification of the intruder.

"Nah," she said. "Dr. Misner couldn't see much. The attacker's head was covered by a balaclava."

After phoning Josie to tell her the news, I rushed to the Celtic Center.

Natalie and a dozen actors sat on metal folding chairs in a circle listening to Erin Starker, the director for the Bloomsday play. As in past years, most were Equity professionals, but the younger roles of Stephen Dedalus, Buck Mulligan, and the lame temptress Gerty MacDowell were filled by talented amateurs drawn from local colleges.

"As most of you know," Erin was saying, "*Ulysses* is the epic novel of a young medical student and a middle-aged ad salesman who encounter each other in Dublin on June 16, 1904. They are wanderers—one in search of a father, the other a son…"

Natalie got up when she saw me motioning for her to join me at the back of the Center.

"What is it?" she demanded as I led her into the boardroom.

"An intruder broke into Emery's room."

"Oh my god!"

"Don't worry. No one was hurt. I doubt Emery even knew what happened. The man fled when Dr. Misner surprised him."

"Did they get a description?"

I shook my head.

She looked out to the center of the main room, where the actors were talking among themselves.

"His parents are with him," I said. "There's no need for you to rush back. I'll stick around to take you to my house when you've finished here. Forget staying at the motel."

She was about to say it was unnecessary, but changed her mind when she saw there was no way I'd let her leave alone.

Chapter 21

*W**ho's that big sumbitch the woman's talkin' to now? I seen him and some dark-haired piece with Denny in that Frog restaurant earlier. I'd best keep an eye on him.*

━━

THE NEXT FEW days passed with no sightings of Grint. The good news was that Emery had begun to show signs of recovery and was removed from the ICU at the end of the week. He still suffered from headaches, slight memory loss, and occasional bouts of violent nausea. The head injury had also restricted blood flow to the part of his brain that controls speech, causing his words to come out garbled. The doctor assured us that he could understand everything being said to him, but, because of the aphasia, Dr. Misner said it might be weeks before Emery could communicate verbally or in writing. Even a simple nod of the head might mean the opposite of what he intended.

His improvement, however, meant Natalie felt comfortable spending more time preparing for the upcoming Bloomsday festivities. Security, always strong at Union Station, was beefed up to add additional support for her. It didn't hurt that the central office was next to the Celtic Center.

We settled into a routine, with Claire helping at the shop after school and coming home with us in the evenings when Natalie went to visit Emery at the hospital.

The more we got to know the girl, the more we began to appreciate just how bright and sweet she could be when not experiencing one of her "episodes." Sometimes she would retreat within herself and her face would take on the same glowing expression as Emery's when he contemplated some mechanical problem or abstract equation.

Josie suspected that both were high-functioning autistics. In Emery's case, it was his single-minded interest in engineering and math, while Claire could become totally absorbed by stories about the paranormal. I could see now that fairies, banshees, and goblins were as real to her as Newton's theory of universal gravitation was to Emery. The child definitely had this thing about owls, and would slip outside to converse with them no matter what time of night.

At Riverrun, she began spending more time in the section that featured folk customs and the supernatural. Alone in the stacks, she would sing softly in that clear, ethereal voice, and Josie and I would stop whatever task we were doing to listen. I suspect that, like me, the girl was prone to hearing voices. Nothing to be concerned about, I figured, as long as she didn't believe, like some modern-day Joan of Arc, that she could turn visions into reality.

Claire was also an easy houseguest, the rare kid who actually volunteered to help with the dishes and laundry. Nonetheless, despite everyone's efforts to be accommodating, my two-bedroom bungalow was beginning to feel as cramped as an industrial feedlot. To make things worse, the always-volatile Natalie was more highly strung than Josie and I had ever seen her. In those few hours when she wasn't at the hospital or the Celtic Center, she quarreled constantly with her daughter.

Her anxiety was understandable, considering that a murderous stalker was lurking about while her fiancé struggled to live, but it was stretching everyone's nerves to the breaking point. Josie's attempts to intervene in the temperamental outbursts only fueled the conflict as Natalie became increasingly jealous of her influence. As for me, I couldn't even seek solace at The Peanut or Fitzpatrick's Galway Pub without incurring the wrath of both women.

Matters weren't helped by the enormous pressure Natalie was under to pull off a successful Bloomsday. It was the Center's major fundraiser and Liam O'Hallo-ran's ludicrous manner of death in front of forty horrified children and adults created a serious image problem for the non-profit. A cell phone video of the poor man's last performance in his Hound of Ulster costume had been taken by one of the older kids and gone viral on the Internet. It was taken down by a mortified parent, but the damage was done—the Celtic Center had become the laughingstock of the town.

While almost everyone claims to have green blood

on St. Patrick's Day, promoting and honoring the great Irish artists, writers, and playwrights was never easy. But over the years, the Center's imaginative and often raucous rendering of Joyce's work had managed to entertain thousands of Kansas citizens who previously thought of Ulysses—if they'd even heard of it—as the greatest novel no one ever read.

Because this was the twentieth anniversary of the event, Natalie had hoped the local public television affiliate would broadcast it. But the station, along with donors who had supported the Center for years, was no longer returning her telephone calls.

Natalie responded as only she could by texting anyone with an O or Mac in their surnames, cold-calling former corporate sponsors, and personally begging priests and the myriad Hibernian societies to not forsake the city's only Irish cultural institution.

And so it went for days.

There was no question of the Phelans' returning to the house on Troost. The landlord, a regular at The Peanut, sympathized with her situation once I explained it. On June twelfth, he let Natalie out of the lease and I leased an apartment for her under my name in Roeland Park, a modest but pleasant suburb on the Kansas side of the line.

There were two other positive developments. Although Emery's injury didn't dispel my obligation to him to make up for the loss of the *Book of Mormon*, Natalie agreed it was better that I have more time to get decent offers for my stock rather than seek a quick loan from Edward Worth's bank. Second, the manager of KCPT called Natalie that same afternoon, June twelfth, reinstating the station's promise to broadcast the Bloomsday play. Things were starting to look downright promising for all concerned.

Josie and I held a farewell barbeque for the Phelans on our patio that night. Looking back on it, I wonder if Porter Grint was watching us even then.

Chapter 22

E arly in the morning on Saturday, the sixteenth of June, the Celtic Center's celebration of Bloomsday kicked off under cornflower blue skies when dozens of cyclists dressed in early twentieth-century Dublin tweeds pedaled their antique messenger bikes through the downtown streets.

Eleven o'clock saw a crowd gathered at Union Cemetery to watch costumed reenactors pretend to bury poor fictional Paddy Dignam with due pomp and ceremony, complete with horse-drawn carriage. In nearby bars and cafés dedicated "Bloomies" ate "with relish the inner organs of beasts and fowls," washed down with pints of Guinness, that "foaming ebon ale."

And somewhere within the bowels of Redemptorist Church, a bedraggled group of volunteers continued to wade through a marathon out-loud reading of the novel they had so optimistically begun twenty hours earlier.

By noon the cyclists had completed their odyssey

and the Dignam mourners were trading their lamentations for drinks in tents set up on the street in front of McCabe Hall. Students from the Art Institute, dressed as characters from the novel in bowler hats, feather boas, petticoats, weskits, and bloomers wandered through the throng while the local opera diva, Sylvia Langan, opened the music performances with a medley of Victorian songs favored by Joyce.

The crowd continued to grow, but it wasn't until Aidan Delahunt took the mike to belt out "Amhrán na bhFiann," Ireland's national anthem—entirely in Gaelic, no less—that things began to take off.

Natalie, with the help of Aidan and a subsidy from Fitzpatrick's Galway Pub, had managed to bring in the top Celtic bands from the region. An extra bonus came in the form of New York's Larry Kirwan, late of Black 47, who was in town on his way to a solo gig in Denver.

Once the music began it didn't take long for the street to become a sea of excited faces, young and old, celebrating their real or imagined Irish cultural heritage in a way that was far different from the drunk fests that have come to characterize too many St. Patrick celebrations around the country.

All credit was due to Natalie and her tiny group of volunteers. They'd pulled it off despite lingering memories of the O'Halloran debacle and the recent turmoil in her life. It shouldn't have surprised me. I'd known Natalie long enough to understand that beneath her fiery passion lay a granite foundation of fortitude.

The sun was dipping under the tree-lined hills to the west when I noticed her standing to the side of the stage. The Doolin Academy Irish Dancers were going through their jigs and reels to thunderous applause. Arms confidently folded in front of her and a satisfied smile creasing her beautiful face, she reminded me of Boadicea, the legendary queen of the ancient Celts, who for one brief, shining moment defeated Britain's Roman invaders.

After the dancers departed the stage, she took the microphone to thank the people, the sponsors, and her volunteers for making the celebration such a success. Then she invited those with tickets for the play to move into McCabe Hall's theater for what always proved to be the best part of the daylong festivities.

The lights dimmed at eight o'clock, and Moira D'Arcy strode onto the stage in her role as narrator. The spotlight shone on her as she intoned:

"The Ormond Hotel restaurant and pub. Just before four o'clock in the afternoon. Bronze by gold, Miss Douce's head by Miss Kennedy's head, over the cross blind of the Ormond bar heard the viceregal's hoofs go by, ringing steel…"

Costumed actors streamed onto the stage and thus began—Brigadoon-like—the audience's magical transport to dirty, lyrical, mercenary-encamped, bordello-infested Dublin, circa 1904; an imaginary slate gray universe in which soldiers, medical students, whores, barflies, and ink-slingers interact with a Jewish everyman in search of home and a son in search of a father.

An hour and a half of theater time later, Leopold Bloom had prevailed over seductive sirens, caught a "refreshing" sight of Gerty MacDowell's ankles, rescued Stephen Dedalus from the perils of Nighttown, and at the end of a very long day, reclined at the foot of his conjugal bed, kissed his wife's rump and fell asleep, presumably content.

The curtain closed and the fourteen actors who had brought James Joyce's colorful Dubliners to life bounded from the wings to be rewarded with a standing ovation. After taking their bows, the cast glided from the stage. However, before the audience headed for the aisles, the narrator reminded them that one more scene remained.

The curtain opened to reveal Natalie in the role of Molly Bloom reclining seductively on an old brass bed. She wore a flimsy cotton skirt, ripped fishnet stockings, and a low-cut bodice. Her face wore a mask of bold-faced shamelessness.

She was the character, no doubt about it—all fire and flowers and flesh—and every eye in that theater locked on her.

At first Natalie portrayed her as a working-class Madame Bovary, an overripe bourgeois wife of questionable reputation, so her soliloquy began quietly, in the sleepy voice of a slightly bemused adulteress who suspects her sexually unsatisfying husband has come home late after a fling of his own. But as the words continued to flow in a languid stream of consciousness, Natalie/Molly evolved into a model of consummate womanhood. Slattern and saint, she was the universal Earth Mother, nature in all its richness.

The monologue was intensely, shockingly personal, and except for a few moralists who scurried out a side door during the earthier passages, the audience remained in their seats, captivated by the unfiltered rendering of what it is like to be a female.

For me, her character became all the women I had known and loved: Carol and Josie and Annie and Alice and Sandra Epstein and Pillow Wilkes and Esme Mackin and Beryl Cowper and little Aronui of the South Island.

Even my own beautiful, alcoholic, abused and abusing mother. God rest her soul.

And first I put my arms around him. Yes. And drew him down to me so he could feel my breasts all perfume.

Yes.

And his heart was going like mad.

And yes.

I said yes, I will.

Yes.

And with that ultimate affirmation of life, the spotlight on Natalie faded to dark. Seconds passed in silence until, like a tempest surging from the eye of a hurricane, the theater erupted with applause.

It went on uninterrupted for ten minutes, maybe more, ending only when Claire climbed onto the stage. After exchanging hugs with her mother, the girl stood to the side, raised her hand for silence and began to sing.

I later learned that the tune "I Dreamt I Dwelt in Marble Halls" was from a nineteenth-century romantic opera favored by Joyce. But it could have been "It's Not Easy Being Green" or the Notre Dame "Victory March" and I wouldn't have noticed. That's because I saw that her eyes had suddenly become focused on something or someone toward the back of the auditorium.

Josie noticed it as well.

Turning as one, we saw that the object of Claire's attention was a stocky, muscular man standing to the left of the double doors under a red exit sign. He wore a mesh trucker hat sporting a Lynyrd Skynyrd logo, a long-sleeved plaid shirt, and faded blue jeans. It was too dark to see his face, but I had no doubt who it was.

Chapter 23

N *ow that's pretty. Real nice. Like an angel singing.*
This girl is definitely coming with me when this is
over. Definitely. Have to put a bag together. Don't
want to worry about not finding any rope in the house. Knife, of
course. Precut some cords, pack tape, and a little mirror.

JOSIE HAD ALREADY DIALED 911 when I hurried up the
aisle with the intent of keeping the man there until the
police arrived. He noticed me, but didn't move, so
intent was he on watching Claire's performance. I
stopped at the top of the stairs, close enough to grab
him should he bolt, yet far enough back to avoid a
swipe of his arms if he had a knife.

It wasn't until Claire finished singing and the
curtain closed that he turned his head to acknowledge
me with a look of utter vacuity. The yellow-gray eyes
studied me as if I were a dead catfish. Under the cap
were an exceptionally meager forehead, a protuberant

nose, grizzled chin whiskers, and razor-thin lips. He smelled of diesel fumes, cigarettes, and dried piss—a human truck stop.

Josie appeared by my side while two friends of mine, Danny Regan and Ed Scanlon, planted themselves in front of the door, ready to pounce should it be necessary.

"Porter Grint?" I inquired.

"What of it?"

His words oozed like bubbles through swamp water.

"The police would like to see you."

"Would they now?" He leaned against a railing. The eyes examined Josie with ratlike interest. "Who made them interested?"

"I think you know."

"I think I don't."

"A whole lot of people."

"I served my time. I'm as free a man as you. Nobody's got anything on me."

"At any rate, here they are now. Try selling your story to them."

Josie and I followed the police car to the Jackson County courthouse, where an hour later, we watched through the one-way glass while Detective Fletcher interrogated Grint. It quickly became apparent that getting him to confess was as likely as getting a snake to warm itself on ice.

He denied everything, but he was a lousy convincer. He said he was in Independence, Missouri, at the time of the fire in Lawrence. He was staying at the Days Inn Motel, but he knew of no one who could vouch for his presence anywhere that day. He claimed to be in Jackson County to visit the original site of the

Garden of Eden, a goal he had set on while in prison. There was something authentic in the way he insisted on this. When asked about the pact to kill Natalie Phelan, his denial was accompanied by an oily smile. He feigned surprise upon hearing of the attempted assault on Emery in the hospital.

"So Emery's here," he said, looking at the mirrored glass as if he could see through it. "I sure would like to talk to him." He paused. "For old times' sake."

The next day I hired an attorney friend to petition Judge Atwell to issue a restraining order preventing Porter from communicating with or coming within a hundred feet of Emery, Natalie, or Claire.

I might as well have asked for a ticket to the moon for all the good it did.

Chapter 24

On the twenty-sixth of June, Josie took a call at noon from a very upset volunteer at the Celtic Center. Natalie hadn't shown up that morning. The Irish Consul General, who had come down from Chicago specifically to get a tour of the place after hearing about the tremendous success of Bloomsday, was cooling his heels in the library. The volunteer had called the hospital, but Natalie hadn't been there, either.

Josie tried Natalie's home and cell phone numbers with the same result the volunteer had. She called the principal's office at Ursuline Academy, who reported that Claire was absent. Josie rushed downstairs to get me. I put aside the book I'd been describing for a new catalog and two minutes later gunned the Jeep for the Phelans' apartment in Roeland Park.

I found the manager skimming leaves from the pool. She ran to her office to get the key. It wasn't necessary. The newspaper lay outside the half-open door. I told the manager to call 911 and walked inside.

There was a teakettle atop a cherry red stove ring. The water in it had evaporated. A leg of the coffee table was broken. A lamp lay on the floor, its shade crushed but the lightbulb still on. A chair in the kitchen had been knocked over. In Claire's bedroom, I found blood smeared on the inside doorknob. I sat on the small bed that was covered by a single sheet and telephoned Detective Fletcher. I called the Days Inn in Independence, only to learn that Grint had checked out the day before. I hung up. I called Josie. I called Buford Higgins. I turned off the stove.

Then I waited for the police to arrive.

While the crime scene technicians busied about the apartment taking measurements and photographs and dusting for prints, I sat in a patrol car describing to the deputy sheriff what I knew. Five minutes later, his radio announced that Grint was in police custody following an altercation at the Kansas City Zoo. A zookeeper had ordered him to stop feeding sunflower seeds to an Amazon parrot, and he responded by shoving the woman against the netting. He ran when she called security, but an alert patrol officer nabbed him on Monkey Island.

"Monkey Island?"

"You heard right," the deputy said. "Lucky for him, the chimps were opposite where he landed. Nasty buggers, chimps."

Back at the Jackson County jail interrogation room, Grint was being more cooperative than he'd been the first time.

Sergeant LaVar Stratten, an enormous Black cop, now asked the questions. He seemed more effective than Detective Fletcher; more patient and understanding. He made nice with Grint. He called him Porter.

He offered him coffee and apologized when the Mormon refused on religious grounds. It was odd seeing the difference in Grint this time around. He looked dog-tired and jumpy. More than worried, he seemed scared.

"This is not good," Josie insisted as we watched behind the glass. "He's had no sleep in a while. That boy's been up all night doing things."

"I was at the zoo all day," he said in response to Stratten's first question. "I ain't been near Kansas."

"Have you seen Mrs. Phelan or her daughter since that night at the school play?"

He answered by not answering.

"Okay, Porter. Where did you see them?"

"At the Irish place."

"In Union Station?"

"If that's what you call it."

"You went in?"

"No. Just stood outside in the hall."

"Why would you do that knowing there was a restraining order? You must have a mighty big crush on her."

Grint grinned. "I ain't queer. And who's to say I wasn't a hundred feet away?"

Stratten grinned back, topped it with an understanding smirk. "We talkin' about the mother or the girl?"

The prisoner raised his chin. "Why are you shakin' me down again? They go missing?"

"You tell me, Porter. Someone broke into their apartment. Made a mess. Bloodstains on a bedroom door. I want to know where they are." The big cop leaned forward, no longer Officer Friendly. "You want

182

me to know where they are. And you most definitely want me to find them alive."

"I can't help you."

"Can't? Or won't?"

Grint reached across the table for a mint Stratten had pushed toward him earlier. His thin fingers peeled off the wrapping paper and popped the candy in his mouth.

"You're not going to find my prints in that apartment, Sergeant. You're not gonna find particles of my hair, no fibers from my clothes, no hint of my DNA. I never been there."

Stratten took a few moments to look into the man's face. I saw what he saw. Porter Grint seemed to believe what he was saying.

"Three of you vowed to kill Natalie Phelan. One's still in a coma, the other is physically incapable. That leaves you. Give me a reason not to believe it isn't you."

"I don't want to harm her."

"I see." Stratten sneered. "You just want to sniff around, peek in on her and her little girl. Harmless fun."

"Yeah," Grint said, his reddened eyes glistening. "For twelve years, it's all I could think of, how I'd disappointed my uncle by getting sent to prison in a stupid fight. I'll admit it, Sergeant, I was ready to honor the oath. That's what I'd been trained to do. But I began to think different once I started readin' my LDS Bible without my uncle looking over my shoulder, guidin' the meanings to fit his way. It took a while and some talk with the prison chaplain, but I finally figured it wasn't what Joseph Smith wanted. Not even

Brigham Young. Sometimes words get twisted funny. People read in them things that aren't real."

He leaned back. Stared into the big man's eyes and said, "I killed that dude in Rock Springs. Still feel bad about it, even though he would've skewered me first if he hadn't been so drunk. But I ain't out to hurt nobody, less'n they come after me."

"Then why did you show up in this neck of the woods?"

"I wanted to see her, to tell her not to worry. Not about me, at least."

"Who should she worry about, then?"

"Cousin Emery, of course." Grint accepted another mint. "Our uncle always thought it would come down to him. Wild-ass that I was as a kid, he knew I'd get waylaid some way, somehow. Emery was Mr. Quiet, not a mean bone in his body, but you should have seen him take to the lessons that last year with Lamar. Nothing could stop him if he believed in something. And he believed more than me or Dennis in that atonement hooey."

I glanced sideways at Josie. Her upper body was rigid as she stared through the glass.

"Why would a guy admit it to the woman he intends to marry?" Stratten asked. "You're going to have to do better than that."

"You asked my opinion. I gave it."

"Okay. Let's say you're tellin' the truth. That leaves Emery, who isn't going anywhere for a long time, and a man with no legs and one arm."

"So you ain't got nothing to worry about."

"If you had wanted to kill her, how would you have done it?"

"We were taught to slit her throat so that the blood would consecrate the ground."

"Any special time or place?"

"That'll be up to the avenging angel."

His grin when he said that was the most repulsive thing I'd seen in a long time.

Josie turned her head to me. Instantaneously, we mouthed, "The Garden of Eden."

Chapter 25

Independence, Missouri, is surrounded by the megalopolis of Kansas City, but its historical significance is just as great as the larger city's. In the late 1840s, the settlement teemed with migrants escaping foreclosures and lost opportunities in the Eastern cities. But for these intrepid dreamers, it was only a way station; a starting point where they hitched their dreams and sole possessions to oxen, horses, and mules for the great treks to California, Santa Fe, and Oregon.

Then came 1849 and the forges, stables, and taverns went into double duty servicing a different clientele, for this was the beginning of the Gold Rush. The apron-skirted mothers, penniless farmers, and bawling children mixed with raffish Europeans, Indian traders, buck skinned mountain men, Indian scouts and squaws, Mexican mule drivers, and fancy ladies—a gathering of sinners and saints of all races, all hopes. For all their differences, they were united in one respect: the desire to find fortune on the other side of the continent. It was nothing less than the incubator of the American West.

Before that, however, another group of pioneers had determined the place to be something far greater. In 1830 a hundred steady, hardworking, and devout pioneers came to the gentle woodland hills and meadows for the purpose of founding a New Jerusalem. There is no direct evidence that Joseph Smith, Jr., officially declared the area to be the site of the Garden of Eden, but Brigham Young said that he had and later LDS leaders agreed. What is certain is that in 1831 Joseph Smith, having received a revelation from an angel, purchased several acres to be the center of the "City of Zion."

At first, their industriousness and piety appealed to the locals, but, as had happened in New York, Ohio, and Illinois, it soon became apparent that the Mormons were not about to coexist with those not of their faith. Before a temple could be built, they were forced to flee to Illinois. In the interim, Joseph Smith was killed, but some of his flock, led by his first wife, Emma, and his son, Joseph Smith III, returned. They established a church separate from what became the "desert Mormons" led by Brigham Young.

I'm not sure what Josie and I expected to find as we drove the ten miles to Temple Lot in Independence. All we knew was that Mormons still believed it to be the epicenter of the Garden of Eden, and we might find some hint as where Natalie and Claire had been taken. What we found on South River Boulevard was not a Garden but a simple stone church on one side of open green space. Opposite it was the magnificent three-hundred-foot stainless steel spire of the Church of Christ Temple and its massive auditorium.

It was getting near dusk, but hundreds of people milled about the grounds, moving in and out of the churches and the other buildings.

"Whoever has Natalie wouldn't risk harming her here," Josie said after we had traversed the seventy-acre perimeter. "It's too open, too busy."

"I agree. But we're not going to get anything else out of Porter. Let's check on Emery."

THE RECEPTIONIST at the desk wasn't going to let us see Emery until Arihi Tuitama showed up to vouch for us.

"He's progressed well, but he's not able to communicate," the nurse said as she led us down the hall to his room. "Please don't stay more than ten minutes."

Emery sat upright in the bed by the window. His eyes brightened and the corners of his mouth arched upward as we entered the room.

"It's good to see you, Emery," I said, pulling up a chair next to him.

Josie kissed him on his forehead then hopped onto a counter next to a washbasin. Arihi began to adjust his intravenous tube.

"We need your help," I told him. "Natalie's gone missing."

Emery's eyes widened. The eighth-inch smile dissolved.

"Claire is gone, too. Someone, we don't know who, intends to fulfill the oath. We thought you might have an idea as to where. Maybe someplace sacred to the *Book of Mormon*? We've been to the area surrounding the Temple Lot, but it doesn't seem possible there. Can you suggest anywhere else?"

The light from the fading sun painted his skin even more ashen. He squinted his eyes and the muscles in his face strained as he tried to move his lips. His jaw dropped an inch, and he uttered something that made no sense. He tried again.

"Ah...on...di..."

His head fell back onto the pillow. A tear formed in the corner of his right eye.

"Try again, Emery. I know it's difficult. Even if the words come out scrambled, we can piece something together. You've got to do this. We need the name of a place near here where the atonement might occur. A holy spot."

"Ah...on...di...mehhh..."

Having finished replacing the saline solution in the intravenous tube, Arihi leaned over my shoulder and whispered, "Perhaps I can help."

I suddenly recalled that she, like her father and hundreds of other Pacific Islanders in the area, was a Mormon.

"Go ahead," Josie urged.

I let Arihi have my chair.

"Brother Emery," she began. "I am Arihi Tuitama, a sister Saint. Tell us again what you know. Let the spirit of the Prophet guide and strengthen you."

Again he raised his head with difficulty. He opened his mouth, took in a great breath, and exhaled. He sagged back into the pillows. Nothing was said. Arihi and I helped him to sit up again. His eyes widened with effort. They were clear and intensely determined.

"Ahhdaaammmm...on..."

"Adam," Josie said, unable to hide her disappointment. "We're back to the Garden of Eden."

"Ahhdamm," he insisted, his eyes locked on Arihi. "...Ond..."

"Let's go," I whispered to Josie. "You're right. We're wasting our time."

Obviously, the trauma that had affected his speech hadn't diminished his hearing. He glared at us as he repeated, "Ahhdamm...ondi..."

"That's it!" exclaimed Arihi. "Adam-ondi-Ahman —meaning the land of God where Adam dwelled in the ancient language. I should have realized it. Adam and Eve journeyed there after being cast from the Garden of Eden. It's a sacred place where Adam, the father of us all, was baptized by the spirit of the Lord and where he received the Holy Ghost and the temple ordinances. After fulfilling the dictates of the Lord, Eve bore Adam's children, and they sacrificed the first of their flocks."

"Sacrificed?"

"There were two altars used by Adam there: the altar of prayer, and the altar of sacrifice where the lamb shall be offered for the sins of the world."

She pulled from her vest pocket a small, heavily thumbed book and read, "Three Nephi, chapter 27, verse 19: 'And no unclean thing can enter his kingdom; therefore nothing entereth into his rest save it be those who have washed their garments in my blood, because of their faith, and the repentance of all their sins, and their faithfulness unto the end...'"

She hesitated.

"Three years before Father Adam died, he met in that valley with his righteous posterity—Seth, Enos, Methuselah, Daniel, and a thousand other high priests —and bestowed upon them his last blessing. When it was over, the Lord appeared and declared him prince, and the others thereafter addressed Adam as the archangel Michael."

"How appropriate," Josie said, glancing at me. "Please tell us this place is within driving distance."

Arihi nodded. "It's up around Gallatin, Missouri, an hour and a half from here. And there's something else…"

"Yes?" I asked, eager to get on my way.

"It may not be important, but tomorrow is June twenty-seventh."

"Meaning?"

"It's the day Governor Ford's militia murdered the Prophet Joseph Smith, Jr."

When I looked at Emery, he was softly pounding his chest with his fist.

Chapter 26

It was five-thirty by the time we got through rush hour traffic and headed up I-35. According to our map, Adam-ondi-Ahman was seventy miles north of Kansas City, just past the Daviess County seat of Gallatin, Missouri.

This section of Northwest Missouri is a great place —if you're a watermelon. Blessed by fertile bottom-land, it is peopled by sturdy conformists who can make Bulgarian undertakers seem like the Merry Pranksters.

As we edged past the city limits, Josie pulled from her bag a pile of documents and books that she had checked out from the LDS Visitors Center in Independence. The first was a handsome blue cloth-covered book three inches thick. Its gilt and blind-stamped title stated it was volume three of The History of the Mormon Church.

Turning to a section from Joseph Smith's diary, Josie read an excerpt dated May 19, 1838. It described how Smith and Sidney Rigdon crossed the Grand River and came to a hill at the base of which they believed to be an ancient Nephite altar of prayer and sacrifice.

"Rigdon!" I exclaimed. "He's the Danite who had inscribed the *Book of Mormon* to Alonzo Stagg."

"Right," Josie said. "Smith dubbed it Tower Hill and said it was where the Prophet Daniel predicted Adam would return to address his people at the day of reckoning. That same afternoon, Smith laid claim to the entire valley, declaring it to be the original site of Adam-ondi-Ahman."

Josie flipped through a few more pages.

"Okay, listen to this," she said excitedly. "The editors write in a footnote that a mound of rocks jutting from a spur at the base of Tower Hill may mark the spot of Adam's grave. They even mention a legend that on certain nights a light illuminates his spirit walking among the rocks."

"Well, there it is," I said, pressing down the accelerator. "We've got to find Tower Hill."

Thirty seconds later, the speedometer topped ninety miles per hour; at about the same time, I noticed the flashing blue and red lights in my rearview mirror.

"Ah, Jesus."

"You can't very well tell him we're on a mission from God," Josie exclaimed. "Floor it!"

"No, no, no, no, no."

I pulled over.

Trooper Buzard reminded me of my old drill instructor—all chin and monosyllables to go with the Smokey the Bear hat.

"License and registration," he demanded.

I found the latter buried under a pile of gas station

receipts, a Michelin guide map, and a tire gauge in the glove compartment.

"Tax receipt."

"Officer, I'm in something of a hurry."

There might have been worse things to say, but I doubt it.

Trooper Buzard tapped his nightstick on my windshield.

"One moment, sir," Josie said as she waded through my car document pack. She finally managed to find it wrapped around an ice scraper next to a deck of old CDs. Reaching across me to hand it to him, she not so gently smacked my privates as a subtle warning to cool it.

He took the documents and went back to his car. An ice age or two later, he returned. The lights were still blazing.

"I clocked you at ninety-three miles per hour in a sixty-five zone."

"If you say so, sir."

"Say so? How fast d'ya think you were going?"

This riled my lawyerly instincts. He hadn't bothered to read me my rights against self-incrimination.

"I prefer not to answer that, sir."

"Hokay."

He pulled out his ticket calculator thing, took forever to punch in the time, the date, and my speed, and pulled out the automatic ticket telling me to appear at the Clay County courthouse on July seventh. Or I could pay a fine of nine hundred dollars, payable to the Clerk of the Court.

"Nine hundred dollars!"

It just blurted out.

"You were in a work zone. Fees double."

Like hell I was.

Buzard—it was easy to drop the honorific—waited for me to say something. I would have, too, but Josie had resumed her grip on my yarbles.

I signed the glowing screen with my finger and handed it back to him.

"You're lucky I didn't haul you in."

"Yes, I am very lucky. Thank you."

Ah, sarcasm; language of the devil. You'd think I'd know better by now.

I started to start the ignition, but his right hand shot in and pulled the key out.

"What the fu—"

"You one of those Mormons?"

"No, sir."

"Do you have a home church, Mr. Bevan?"

"Excuse me?"

"A home church."

"Uh, Our Lady of Perpetual Sorrow and Agony."

"Sounds Catholic."

"It does, doesn't it?"

"Attend regularly?"

By now Josie saw where this was going. The newspaper had reported a rash of religious proselytizing by law enforcement officers in western Missouri lately, something to do with a wowser named Officer Billy Ray Schweiker who, when he wasn't issuing tickets or scraping victims off highways, hosted a radio show called Policing for Our Lord.

"Trooper Buzard," she whispered loudly. "Perhaps I can answer that."

He stuck his head through my window. The mingled odor of Red Man chew and Old Spice filled the Jeep.

"Go right ahead, little lady."

"You see, Trooper, Michael and I are engaged to be wed next month. And, well, I'm of the Baptist faith and he…he's a crappie crunch…uh…Michael was raised, through no fault of his own, in the Roman Church. We were on the way to Gallatin to get my pastor's blessing. It is my sincere hope that the Reverend Mott will convince Michael to accept the rightful Jesus Christ as his savior. But we are running late and the Reverend, being an impatient man…"

"Which way you leanin'?" he snarled at me.

I took Josie's hand from my crotch and pressed her fingers to my lips.

"I have seen the light, Trooper Buzard, and shall follow the righteous path forevermore."

He took off his aviator sunglasses to better examine my soul.

I obliged with a look so contrite it would have made Mary Magdalene jealous.

"All right then. Blessings to you both." He handed me back the keys.

"And the ticket, Trooper?"

"Don't push your luck, asshole."

We called Buford Higgins five times during the next twenty minutes, getting his voice mail every time.

An hour later, I turned off the interstate onto a series of ever smaller rural byways bordered by ripening fields of soybeans where algae-choked ponds and crumbling barns dotted the landscape. Despite the traffic ticket, I set my cruise control a nickel over the speed limit, slowing only when approaching the ramshackle towns of single-pump gas stations, shade tree repair shops, and dilapidated shacks. Ten miles after passing through Altamont, we came to the outskirts of Gallatin. Just past the town was a sign directing us to Highway 13, but I would have missed the turn to it had Josie not shouted for me to pull over.

The Jeep rattled over the shoulder rumble strips as I guided it to a full stop.

"There." She pointed to a two-lane blacktop road on the other side of a short wood bridge spanning a shallow culvert. "See that?"

She was referring to a nondescript wooden marker that was nearly hidden by the state highway sign. It was no larger than two feet by three and there was nothing official about it. Pale yellow letters three inches high on a brown background declared Adam-ondi-Ahman to be in the vicinity. A thin arrow drawn next to the words hinted—but only just—that we should proceed north on the undulating lane that had no business being called a highway.

It was only after I backed up and entered the road that another modest sign, similar in color and size, but declaring a distance of 3.8 miles, confirmed we were on the right path to where God had expelled the progenitors of all humanity.

The sun was beginning to dip below the tips of the forested hills when we came to our destination. The sign to the entrance declared "Adam-Ondi-Ahman—Historic Site of the Church of Jesus Christ of Latter-day Saints" in eight-inch letters of bright Swedish blue and sunflower yellow. Not exactly a Vegas-style welcome, but far more definitive than the earlier enigmatic posts.

Our initial impression as we pulled left on gravelly Koala Road was surprise at the minimalist markings for a site that the Mormon texts declared to be of primary significance. After all, the Latter-Day Saints, as evidenced by their grand marble temples scattered throughout the world from Samoa to South Africa, were not known for hiding their light under a bushel basket. Whether or not this was a pilgrimage site, I had the unmistakable feeling that visitors—Mormon and gentile alike—were welcome to drop in for a look but not to overstay the privilege.

The white-fenced acreage extending from the road up to the overlook was in a mostly natural state, devoid of buildings, signage, and trash. The gravel roads threading through the area were well maintained with none of the moon-crater-sized potholes that characterized Highway 13. The grass was freshly cut and the weeds bordering the fences were under control, but there was nothing to suggest the abundant, immaculately landscaped flower gardens one associates with the Mormons.

I didn't expect to find a Branson-style visitor's center where dazzled tourists could buy postcards depicting biblical scenes, posters of blond-bearded prophets, and paperweights in the shape of ancient stone altars. But the total lack of commercialism seemed to be a concentrated effort to downplay what some might consider embarrassing church doctrine. While Adam and Eve are inescapably real people in Mormon theology, Joseph Smith's decree that God banished them from paradise to rural Missouri is something that even literal-believing Saints have trouble wrapping their heads around. The site can't be ignored—although the more liberal-leaning Community of Christ pretty much has—but neither do the LDS leaders think it should be exposed to public scrutiny any more than is necessary.

Driving up the hill, we came upon a young woman

wearing a white blouse and blue ankle-length skirt. A red bandanna tied around her hair controlled all but a few wandering blond curls above the back of her sunburned neck. She carried an orange bag in which to put litter—something we had yet to observe since turning off the highway. When we offered her a lift, she declined, saying she was engaged in her mission work.

"What else do you do here?" Josie asked.

"Mostly this," she answered. "I'm also in charge of the two public bathrooms. On weekends, a handful of us try to control weeds on the surrounding farms. I know it sounds mundane, but I turned down a mission in Italy for this place. I think it's kind of cool."

"How about a guided tour?"

She looked at me as if I'd asked her to strip. "Tower Hill is just over a mile from here," she said after realizing I was serious. "It's where the Prophet meant to build the temple, and you can still see the rocks meant for the foundation. Below it, next to a dirt road, is the Preacher Rock. Follow the signs and the white fence posts. You'll want to watch out for rattlers, chiggers, and ticks when you get there."

"Anything else we should know about?" Josie asked.

She looked at us strangely. "Only that there will be a full moon tonight. You'd best not linger too long because the gate closes at dusk."

With that, she nodded a brisk farewell and continued her futile search for candy wrappers.

A dusty mile and a half later, I drove up a steep incline to park in a small visitors' lot surrounded by oak and thorny locust trees. We got out of the Jeep and walked along a dark, winding trail flanked by overgrown thickets until arriving at a triangular-shaped grove. A plaque confirmed it to be the top of Tower Hill, where in 1832, Joseph Smith urged his followers to build a temple. A dozen flat stones of varying bulk lay scattered as if dropped haphazardly by a giant. At the far end of the spot was a bluff above the verdant Grand River Valley.

With the last rays of the sun christening the clouds in pink and gold, I followed Josie to the overlook's edge. To say that either one of us was religious is like saying Porky Pig is articulate, but I can't deny being touched at that moment by something spiritual; something that felt immensely greater than either of us.

Even if the site didn't seem as plausible as somewhere along the Euphrates, I couldn't help but feel the presence of the father and mother of us all; those ancient stand-ins for all our sins and hopes who were cast from Eden into a dreary world of sorrow, pain, lust, hunger, and constant striving, only to have their miserable existence culminate in death.

The place certainly wasn't the supposed paradise from which they'd been driven, but it wasn't exactly Death Valley. On the edge of the mowed grass were thistles, thorn trees, dead and broken branches. Sweat bees swarmed around us. I pulled two ticks from Josie's neck and swatted at chiggers gnawing my ankles. Then I saw another path, this one leading down the bluff a hundred yards or so to a flat boulder, much larger than the stones behind us. Beyond it was a heavily rutted dirt service road, and a shallow meadow and the beginning of more forest. To the north lay a broad swath of cultivated bottomland.

We started down the trail in the increasing darkness, tripping over loose rocks and pushing aside brambles and low-hanging branches until we came to the oblong boulder that must have been what the Mormon girl called Preacher Rock. The thing looked as if it had broken off from a meteor. It was gray-black, fifteen feet long, ten feet wide at its center, and nearly three feet thick. Flat as an aircraft carrier, it lay perfectly balanced upon another slightly less massive white stone.

The velvet night had descended upon us, cloaking us in its cold arms, making our surroundings seem haunted and desolate.

Josie ran her hands along the side of the stone. She looked over her shoulder at me. "If I didn't know better, I'd say this really was once an altar."

"For prayer or sacrifice?"

With a shrug, Josie pulled out the pamphlet, turned on her penlight, and read:

"'Smith's surveyors discovered a large stone. When Joseph examined it he said it was the remains of an altar built by Father Adam and upon which he had offered sacrifices. When the angel of the Lord asked Adam why he offered sacrifice, Adam replied that the Lord had commanded him to do it and that blood of bulls and goats and lambs should be spilt upon the altar to symbolize the great and last sacrifice which should be offered up for the sins of the world....'"

She looked up. "Sure sounds like—"

But before she could finish, I flung her to the ground, and we scrambled on our bellies to hide behind a pair of thornbushes.

Chapter 27

The approaching lights reached the top of the dirt road in front of us before sweeping on.

"That's got to be them," I said, jumping to my feet. But by then, Josie had already started running after the zigzagging red taillights.

I soon caught up with her, grabbing her elbow to keep us out of sight of the rearview mirrors. Periodic "No Trespassing" postings indicated we had entered an area beyond the official Adam-Ondi-Ahman public access road. The potholes kept the SUV's pace slow enough for us to maintain surveillance for a couple of miles, but when the vehicle headed up a steep hill, we lost contact. Gasping for breath at the top, we searched ahead in vain for the lights.

"We're close," Josie said. "This road is too much of a mess to connect to the outside. It must end soon."

But she was wrong, because after jogging another half mile, we came to an open gate beyond which was nothing to indicate it was LDS territory anymore. We kept moving until we got on an asphalt lane that led us into the sad little town of Garmason.

The faded welcome sign proclaimed it to have a population of forty-five, but that seemed an overstatement for a place where tarpaper sheds and mostly abandoned houses lined the unlit, disintegrating streets. City Hall was a tiny cinder block building that sat across from Duly's Garage, a boarded-up gas station that likely hadn't serviced a car since the Vietnam War. A Lion's Club banner hung lopsidedly on one hinge, blocking half of the Future Farmers of America emblem beneath it.

At the edge of the village, someone had converted a shipping container into a home. A mangy dog sprawled in front of it. Chained to a stake, the pitiful thing stared at us balefully, too worn out or distrustful of humans to even bother barking. The village was almost completely dark except for two or three dwellings where the flashing glare of television sets illuminated the otherwise darkened rooms. The only structure that showed any signs of care was the First Baptist Church.

"There," Josie said, pointing to the beams of a vehicle slowly winding up tight curves on a forested hill in the distance. We kept moving, getting on a gravel road that rose out of town. Surrounded by the foliage, we could no longer see the SUV, but it didn't matter because twenty minutes later, our instincts told us we had arrived.

The approach to the house was little more than a rock-strewn series of muddy ruts that branched off the road and wended toward a stand of tall cottonwoods. Behind the trees, a yellow gleam flickered between the leaves like a beacon to our destination. We walked ahead with caution, following tire tread marks that twisted and turned around and sometimes over fallen logs, saplings, and discarded appliances. Overgrown thornbushes clung to a rotted fence post.

Finally, we came within sight of a narrow, two-story weather-beaten farmhouse straight out of *Psycho*. The windows through which the light shone were exaggeratedly vertical, indicating high ceilings within. Moving to the cover of the trees, we advanced to a point adjacent to the small clearing in front of the house. In the grass behind the structure was a tractor that hadn't worked a field for half a century. Parked haphazardly near it were four mud-splattered vehicles. The Chevrolet Monte Carlo carried Kansas tags, but the two pickups and the SUV had been registered in Colorado, Utah, and Arizona respectively.

"I'm going for a closer look," I said to Josie. "Keep calling Buford. He's the only one who can convince the police as to what's happening and that we'll need reinforcements."

"Even if I contact him, he won't be able to find us in this area."

"His GPS will get him to Koala Road. Meet him at the entrance and guide them here."

It meant she would have to jog four or five miles in the dark to reach the Jeep and drive back to the main entrance, but there were no other options. I headed for the house without waiting to see if Buford answered his phone.

The night being warm and humid, I found the first window open and peered in. A lit Coleman propane lantern hung on a hook from the ceiling. Its eerie yellow glow showed a hoary-bearded Methuselah with a deeply lined face sitting at a plain wooden table. He wore a checkered lumberjack shirt through which a few limp hairs poked. Filthy woolen trousers hung on him like burlap sacks.

He bent his head over an open book as if in prayer. Next to the book was a long steel knife with a bone handle. A Smith & Wesson revolver rested in a leather shoulder holster under his left arm.

Even before I noticed the cylindrical oxygen tank leaning upright by his chair, I could see that he was desperately ill. As if to further confirm this, he was suddenly seized by a horrible, racking cough.

Lamar Stagg, I realized. The patriarch madman in the flesh.

Two other men, mid-thirties maybe, one long and lean with a freckled fox face, the other short and chunky with thick blue jowls. The latter seemed the more dangerous of the two, the kind of charmer who, if he shook your hand, you'd want to count your fingers. They stood in front of an empty fireplace speaking in muted voices so as not to disturb the elder Stagg. What looked to be a semiautomatic AR-15 Bushmaster lay on the mantel between them. Hanging above the weapon was a calendar featuring a photograph of the Angel Moroni atop a temple. The head, neck, and upper chest of the holy messenger were framed by a full moon.

I struggled to hear what the two men were saying and heard snippets about its being about time to get on with things. Upstairs a radio played Merle Haggard's "Silver Wings." Someone in a back room sneezed. I moved along the east side of the house to the next window, where I saw Porter Grint sitting in a cane chair with his back to me. His shoulders were slumped forward as if he were asleep.

I kept moving until reaching a window in the middle section of the house. Peering in, I saw that the long horizontal room was dark except for a wedge of light seeping under the closed door. It was enough to detect the outline of Claire dressed in her school uniform. She lay face down on the steel springs of a cast-iron bed. Her wrists were tied to the vertical bars of the frame behind her head so that her arms extended back and upward. Because her face was turned toward the wall, I couldn't tell if her eyes were open, but her chest seemed to rise and fall at a faster than normal rate. A dingy cloth gag that might have been a T-shirt was wrapped around her mouth.

I tried to open the window, but it was either locked or jammed. Claire's head moved slightly at the noise. I tapped lightly on the glass. She reacted again. I repressed the urge to call to her.

A wise decision, because the door suddenly opened to reveal Grint standing in the doorframe with a flashlight. He glanced over his shoulder before shutting the door behind him. He approached the bed, stopped at the head of it, and shone the beam up and down the length of the girl, slowly.

Sprinting to the rear of the house, I found the back door was locked, but not the window. I raised it and crawled into a storage room filled with garden tools, pots, and burlap bags stinking of fertilizer. A Dutch door separated it from the area where Claire was. I opened the top an inch or two. Grint had moved so that he was sitting on the edge of the bed. He leaned over Claire, the stubbles of his beard brushing her forehead. I could hear her panting.

"You'd best be nice to me, cutie," I heard him say. "'Cuz I'm the only reason you're still alive."

He prodded the girl's hip with the flashlight while his other hand reached for the bottom of her skirt. He slowly began to lift it.

I grabbed a rusted sickle hanging on the wall next to me, fully intending to slide stealthily into the room to dispatch the would-be molester or die in the attempt.

It didn't work out that way.

For one thing, the metal part of the sickle fell onto my foot, leaving me clutching a rotted wooden handle. For another, the bottom half of the door was locked from the other side and wouldn't open.

Finally, any heroics on my part—at least for the moment—proved unnecessary when the opposite door to Claire's room crashed open to reveal a tall, broad-shouldered figure filling the portal.

"That's enough," the quiet voice commanded. "Step away from her. Now."

I couldn't see his features. The light from the hallway cast him in shadow, but soon despair and hope, certainty and doubt, warred within me even as Grint withered before the next blast of words.

"When I give an order, it's to be done as I say. Do you understand?"

Grint rose from the bed slowly, reluctantly.

"But Lamar has promised to seal her to me," he whined.

The other man took three brisk steps forward, smacked Grint across the face with his left hand, and growled, "Only after the atonement is satisfied. You will not defile our holy mission before."

Grint rubbed his cheek, made a very slight movement behind his back, and drew out a snub-nosed pistol.

"I ain't takin' no more orders from you. I was the chosen one."

"You forfeited that right a long time ago in Wyoming," the tall man replied calmly. He paused to readjust Claire's skirt. "Now, put that away. We've got important work to do. Each of us."

Grint didn't move. Then in a voice as flat as western Kansas, he asked, "You ever hear things?"

"Things?"

"You know, voices. Like in your head."

"From the Holy Spirit?"

"No," he said. "Most definitely not that."

"Can't say I have, Port."

"You're lucky."

The other man laughed ironically. "I wouldn't say that."

"You shouldn't have hit me," Grint muttered.

"It was necessary to bring you to your senses. The girl has bewitched you."

"I ain't loved nobody before."

"Get a grip on yourself. When we finish our work, you can have her for all eternity."

Grint started to respond, but a sudden, startling sob engulfed him. He lowered the weapon and kneeled beside the bed.

A minute passed before the other man placed his hand on Grint's trembling shoulder.

"Come away, Port," he said gently.

And with that, Grint dutifully rose to follow his cousin from the room.

I stored the shock of seeing Dennis Dietz's upright appearance in the cabinet of my brain that handles such things. A brighter sleuth who knew about biomechatronic limbs might have foreseen his ability when it would have made a difference. I had no excuse, having been told by Detective Fletcher what his old patrol partner had attempted after losing both legs.

Where Officer Carter had eventually given up, a man like Dietz would have succeeded. Perhaps Denny was mentally tougher than the cop who had killed himself. But the marine not only had the superior expertise of military doctors; he also enjoyed the all-important psychological support of other severely injured peers. None of them would have laughed at the progressive use of "shorties."

There were other hints I had missed that would disqualify me from being confused with Monsieur Poirot—and please, don't all you smarty pants mention the name of the company on Dietz's calling card. Biomechatronic Solutions, indeed.

For instance, when I telephoned Dietz from Detective Fletcher's office, he sounded groggy, as if I'd awakened him. But while it was around one a.m. in Kansas City, it was merely eleven in the Golden State, where no one over eight years old hits the hay until after the first half of *The Tonight Show* with Jimmy Fallon. Furthermore, all that traveling by air and renting a van would have been extremely difficult for him, particularly given the time frame. He'd never left the Midwest after arriving in Lawrence.

Brilliant deductions, Bevan—except they only came to mind after the cows had left the proverbial barn.

But I digress.

Now there was work to do. I reached through the upper half of the door to unlock the lower one. After picking up the blade of the rusty sickle, I crept into the room, raised one of the windows for an avenue of escape, and moved to the bed.

Claire's eyes were wide open and staring, terrified and unsure who this new intruder in the dark might be.

I leaned over so that she could see my face.

"Keep still," I whispered as I untied the gag covering her mouth. "After I cut the ropes, head into the woods and keep going until you get to the highway. Josie should be near the entrance of the park. And don't worry about your mother. I'm not leaving without her."

She was a tough kid. Her only response was to nod.

Moving behind the head of the iron bedstead, I began to draw the curved blade back and forth on the inch-and-a-half-thick knotted climbing rope that bound her wrists. It was slow work. Five minutes poured into ten. Twice I heard footsteps in the hall. Once I heard two men arguing about who would take the kid for a bathroom break. I kept sawing. Claire kept quiet despite the blade nicking her wrists. Couldn't be helped.

At last the cord broke.

"Go, Claire," I hissed, "and Godspeed to you."

She disappeared through the opened window while I headed in the opposite direction for the hallway and a very uncertain future.

Chapter 28

I cracked open the door a few inches, twisted my head sideways and peered down an empty hall. Voices could be heard coming from the living room. I started to step out when I heard a toilet flush. I closed the door and waited until the steps retreated. Without bothering to look this time, I entered the hall and glided past two rooms on the right until coming to what looked like a closet.

It was about four feet wide and two feet deep inside. Old cardboard boxes stuffed with cotton dresses and men's work clothes covered half the floor. A rusty double-barreled shotgun leaned in a corner. Good news, if it was functional. There was a box of shells sitting next to it. But the shells contained No. 9 bird-shot—good for killing birds, but not effective for stopping a determined foe beyond fifteen feet.

I loaded the gun and was about to look for a better vantage point when I noticed the outline of a trapdoor on the ceiling. A frayed rope hung from it.

I set the gun down, shoved the clothes boxes aside

to allow more room, and tugged on the cord. The ladder unfolded easily enough, but the steps were treacherously rotted. Keeping my insteps wedged against the sides, however, I made it up to a small attic space. Its sole purpose was to accommodate a huge house fan circa 1920. Light and sound from the living room below filtered through its thick mesh screen.

After several tense minutes, I succeeded in squeezing on my knees to a spot where my head was half a foot from the blades. It was hotter than Hades and it stank of bat droppings and mouse piss, but I couldn't have asked for a better observation post of the living room. After settling on my haunches, I looked down to see and hear Dietz addressing his uncle. There was no sign of Grint.

"You shouldn't have promised to seal the girl to him," Dietz said.

Lamar Stagg, a long-limbed, broad-shouldered ancient, rose from the table. He was gaunt and wheezy and even from my perch, I could hear his dentures clack, but I figured he could be a very tough hombre for the short term. That wild-eyed bearded face showed the feral defiance of a timber wolf that may have been past its prime but was still leader of the pack. He'd die hard.

"For sure we made a mistake," I heard the old man say. "But Port needs a wife. With that ugly mug and being a little soft in the head he ain't likely to get a prize heifer on his own. Let him keep her under lock and key in Mexico. She won't go tellin' on us."

I noticed the mechanical hitch in Dietz's gait as he moved to his uncle's side. He said firmly, "It's too risky. I hate it, but we can't let her be a witness."

The uncle grunted. He walked over to the couch

and picked up a stuffed pillow embroidered with the words Courage—Wisdom—Serenity.

"I helped cause the problem," he said. "Guess it's up to me to put a stop to it. We'll find him somebody else."

"You're going to suffocate her?"

"Why waste a bullet?"

The codger headed into the hallway. I waited with a mixture of concern and satisfaction for the volcanic eruption sure to follow when he discovered the bird had flown.

I wasn't disappointed.

"She's escaped! Seth! Jacob!"

The two men rushed from elsewhere in the house to join Lamar and Dietz in the main room.

"Find her!" Lamar shouted. "I don't care if you have to shoot the little bitch. Just get her."

Grint stumbled frantically down the broad staircase. He had a stricken look as he watched the two armed men dash from the house.

"What'd you tell them?" he demanded of his uncle. "Shoot her? That ain't right."

Dietz stepped between them.

"Is the woman secure?" he asked Grint.

"What?"

"Natalie Phelan, you fool. Still secure?"

"Yeah," Grint answered distractedly as he headed for the door. "The girl's mine. I'm gonna find her."

Lamar grabbed him by the shoulders. "You'll stay here."

"But they'll kill her."

"Yes, God willing."

"No, Uncle! You promised her to me. All I've done for you…"

Dietz calmly addressed his distraught cousin. "That girl's the least of our problems. She didn't get loose on her own. Forget her. Let the boys handle it."

Grint wasn't listening.

"Get upstairs, boy, and bring the woman down," Lamar ordered. "There's no time to waste. It's almost midnight and the day of reckoning is at hand."

"Not until I've found her!" Grint screamed.

Pulling from his uncle's grasp, he sprinted for the front door, knocking Dietz to the floor.

Dietz, no longer so composed, struggled to his feet. He joined his uncle on the porch to helplessly watch Grint disappear into the woods.

As prompts to action go, there wasn't going to be a better opportunity for yours truly. With Porter and the two Danite henchmen chasing Claire, the present opposition was an old man dependent on an oxygen tank and a triple amputee. The birdshot should do just fine if I could get close enough.

I slid back down the ladder, picked up the gun, and rushed into the room to position myself next to the front door. The two remained outside for a few more minutes while that gotch-eyed, sanctimonious uncle uttered some very un-Mormon-like curses concerning his uncontrollable nephew.

His curses got even bluer when he and Dietz returned inside to find themselves staring into the double barrels of what my former barista used to call the "boom stick."

"Gentlemen," I said, channeling Daniel Craig. "We're going upstairs to get Mrs. Phelan, and then—"

And then my brains became a bucket of butter.

I staggered like a back-alley drunk, the shotgun dangling uselessly at my side. Somehow turning to confront the assailant, I raised a hand in a feeble effort to retaliate, only to catch an iron fist in my solar plexus. I made a faint gurgling sound before collapsing to my knees.

Nauseous and gasping but not entirely out, I gazed up at the broad walnut-colored face just long enough to reflect on yet another of life's not-so-amusing ironies.

Then Stormin' Norman Tate drop kicked me into unconsciousness.

Chapter 29

I awoke tied to a spindle-back chair at the end of the table in the living room. My head felt as if the top had been unscrewed and molten lead poured into it. My whole body ached, particularly my chest where Tate's fist landed, but nothing felt broken. The aroma of coffee brewing clashed with the stench of propane gas from a camping stove.

I didn't remember why I was there or why my head hurt. An old man whose skin had a sickly greenish hue and a younger man with an eye patch sat across from me. They spoke quietly to each other until the older one had a coughing fit. There was something strange about the younger man's arm that extended beneath the right sleeve of his polo shirt. A hefty, darker-skinned brute stood behind him.

Through a tall window, I saw thick cumulus clouds blanketing the sky. For an instant, however, they cleared, allowing silvery moonlight to infiltrate the dirt-smudged panes. When the clouds regained control, the brief radiance seemed like the last gasp of a cold, solitary object.

My head swiveled back to the table where the *Book of Mormon* lay spread open to the front page. My eyes focused on an inscription below the title. It was signed by someone named Alonzo Stagg.

I glanced up and studied the faces of the men. They'd stopped talking. I saw the strange arm move to pick up the book. It brought everything into focus again. For better or worse, the fog cleared.

Dietz was the first to realize I'd regained my senses.

"You shouldn't have been so keen on finding us," he told me. "I'm afraid you're about to become CD."

I think it was his using that abbreviation for collateral damage that replaced my trepidation with white-hot anger. CD—sounds like "seedy"—was the euphemism senior officers used in Iraq to describe our deadly mistakes involving noncombatants.

"Like Eulalia Darp?" I said. My voice sounded strange, as if it had emerged from a deep well. "Why did you kill her, Denny? You could have afforded our price."

"That was his doing," he said, nodding toward Tate. "The night before I arrived in Lawrence, he saw a chance to make his fortune." Dietz paused. "Right, Norm?"

"Yeah," Tate snarled. "The sour old bitch treated me like a Tipi Tom, even worse than those fraternity pricks. I'd been sneakin' things out of the house for years, but she was gettin' wise to it. When I heard she had a buyer coming for that Mormon book, I figured it might as well be me making big money."

"Whose body was by the door?"

"Had to cover my ass," he said, grinning. It was

remarkable how evil Tate looked after seeming so affable when we had first met in Lawrence. "So I killed a drunk Wahoo 'bout my size under the Kaw bridge, where there's plenty of bums to choose from. Drove his body to Darp's house, picked up the Mormon book and a few other things, then lit the match."

His eyes shone. "Ho-ah! Those oil lamps and all that paper sure made a fine bonfire."

"Take it easy," Dietz cautioned the Indian. Turning back to me, he explained, "Tate called me shortly after I arrived at the airport. Didn't say who he was, but made it clear he had what I wanted. I was watching the news report of the fire at the very moment I listened to him on my cell phone. Either I pay him for the book or someone else gets what belonged to us Staggs. It was a no-brainer."

"Especially since I only asked a hundred grand for it," Tate said.

"To be paid after our mission is complete," Dietz reminded him.

"But it ain't all I done. You wouldn't have gotten this far without my muscle."

"So," I said to Dietz, "you sent him to kill Emery in the hospital."

"Of course. Much as I wanted to finish him myself, it wasn't feasible. Norm botched that one, but he managed to grab the Phelans while you and the police were busy watching Porter."

"Maybe I should get a bonus, huh?" Tate said.

Dietz stood silent for a moment. Dragging metallic fingers slowly across his chest, he said, "You'd have a better case if you hadn't taken the girl, too."

"Grint told me not to come back without 'em both. Blame him."

The artificial hand returned to his side.

"Never mind. What's done is done. If you help us finish without further annoyance, I think another five thousand is fair. Don't you, Uncle?"

Lamar cleared a wad of phlegm from the back of his throat and spit it on the floor. The old man shrugged indifferently.

"Damn, that's what I like to hear!" Tate exclaimed. "You want me to look for the kid? I'll finish her right nice."

Porter Grint, who had returned with the other two after unsuccessfully scouring the woods, was still steaming mad. He rushed up to Tate and growled, "You keep your redskin ass away from her."

"I don't take shit from *wasichus* like you," Tate spit back.

"That's enough," Dietz barked. "We have plenty of work to do before this night's over. Seth, Jacob, load up the trucks. Take Tate with you. And you, Port, bring Mrs. Phelan downstairs."

Lamar closed the *Book of Mormon*. "I'll get the garments."

Grint and the other men left on their assignments while the old man ambled down the hall.

"I don't expect you to understand," Dietz said when we were alone.

"What you're doing has nothing to do with your religion."

The blank look in his eye confirmed there was no chance my words would have any effect. Whether due to his uncle's insidious brainwashing, a severe case of PTSD, or a true belief in the righteousness of an abhorrent family legacy, Denny Dietz was as mad as my great-aunt Lucy, the self-proclaimed Road-Kill Pie Queen of Alma, Kansas.

Our staring contest ended when Lamar came back with several white robes draped over his arm. The Danite named Seth also returned to report the vehicles were loaded. Suddenly, a ruckus at the top of the stairs got everyone's attention. I twisted my head as far as I could to see Grint struggling to control Natalie.

She was dressed in a full-length white gown. The right sleeve was spotted with dried blood. They had tied up her hair in a chignon that exposed the nape of her neck. Her arms were bound by a thick hemp rope and her mouth was taped shut, but her legs were free. I figured Grint had untied them in the mistaken belief that she would listlessly descend on her own, thereby saving him the trouble of carrying her.

But the lady hadn't lost her spunk. She kneed Grint's groin repeatedly before Seth ran up the stairs to help him. She thrust a bare foot at this guy, too, but he caught it before it did any damage. Finally able to grasp her legs and shoulders, the two men half carried, half dragged her down the steps, still kicking.

It wasn't until she saw me tied up in the chair that Natalie stopped struggling. I didn't want her to lose hope, so I did the only thing I could do to buck up her spirits.

"Claire got away!" I yelled at the top of my lungs.

It brought the desired gleam back to her eyes, while earning me an ear slap from Uncle Lamar that still makes it hard for me to hear whenever Josie asks me to take out the trash.

Chapter 30

W hile the Stagg relatives went off to don their sacred white robes, Seth and Jacob carried Natalie to the pickup with the Colorado license plates. I watched them toss her into the back, then someone handed Tate a shovel. After dumping it in the trunk of his Chevrolet, he frog-marched me to the car and shoved me in with it. Before the hatch closed, I watched Dietz, Porter, and Lamar climb into the SUV with the Arizona plates. Seconds later I heard the engines roar to life and the three vehicles pulled from the driveway onto the dirt road.

A mile or so later it became clear that I wasn't enti-tled to witness Natalie's sacred atonement for the crime of Governor Ford. I felt Tate steer the car off the road onto what felt like soft turf. He turned off the engine and came back to open the trunk. I sat up and saw that we were on the edge of woods, twenty meters from the road.

There's no use trying to explain the feeling of

dread that enveloped me as I watched the red taillights of the other vehicles fade in the distance. I'd realized my life was forfeit ever since regaining consciousness in the farmhouse, but I'd clung to the hope of somehow saving Natalie as I had her daughter. Now, with the Chevrolet stopped in this isolated spot, it became frighteningly clear that both our fates were sealed.

A low fog rose from the fields, thickening the darkness.

"Git out," Tate ordered, motioning with a .357 Magnum.

I climbed unsteadily from the trunk, the combined effect of apprehension and having likely been concussed. When I was on my feet again, he reached in the trunk to pull out the shovel.

"We're goin' over there," he said, turning back to me. Don't make trouble or you'll get it in the knees. I'd hate to have to drag you."

I stumbled forward, feeling the morose hostility of Tate as he led me to a grim patch of ground covered by greasy clay and scant grass.

Beyond this was a large, dank bog. Narrow streamlets lined with heather and delicate reeds crisscrossed its algae-covered surface. The stagnant water teemed with hovering mosquitoes and the incessant piping of bullfrogs. For an instant, I thought a blue light danced across it, but the quivering radiance left no reflection in the waters. It was as if all my nightmares had come to roost there.

If you ever wondered how those poor souls captured in the Middle East by a heartless enemy could stoically face their execution, the answer from my experience in that fetid grove is simply this: The specter of Death, voluptuous and multiple-limbed, had already pressed her anesthetizing arms around them before they knelt. The slash of the knife they wouldn't feel or the gunshot they would never hear had become an anticlimactic afterthought.

Comforting image, don't you think?

Well, not for me. I wasn't in the Middle East. And although I hadn't a clue how I was going to resist, I had no intention of going "gentle into that good night." For one thing, being left to rot in an unmarked hole feasted upon by insects, never to be discovered or properly mourned had little appeal for me. In fact, it really, really, really pissed me off; which in my case usually trumps the paralyzing effects of terror if there's an ounce of a chance to escape. For another, Josie Majansik was infinitely sexier than the Dark Angel, its plethora of sybaritic arms and legs notwithstanding. And—as if I needed added incentive—so was Natalie Phelan, who, I reminded myself, was in immediate need of rescuing.

It was Norman Tate's pride that offered me that chance. The proud Native American wasn't about to dig a grave while he had someone else to do it for him.

"For you," he said, tossing the shovel at my feet. "Hold out your arms."

Keeping the gun on me with one hand, he used a knife to cut the rope with the other. When he ordered me to pick up the shovel I didn't hesitate, figuring the odds of my survival had just edged up a notch. My arms were free and I had a weapon.

Except Stormin' Norman was no blockhead. He kept a twenty-foot distance between us.

"Dig," he said. "Three feet by seven. Don't have to be deep."

"You sure about this, Norm?"

"Dead sure. A hundred thousand dollars sure. Plus that little bonus and a free pass to Honduras."

"And I'm Michael Jordan."

"Uh-huh."

He raised the gun, pulled back the hammer.

"Dig," he repeated.

I outlined a nice neat rectangle in the clay. "They aren't going to pay you."

"C'mon, hurry up."

"You know too much, Norm. I bet Jacob and Seth doubled back and are watching us right now." I pointed the end of the shovel toward the trees. "They're in that thicket waiting for you to finish me so they can get you next."

"Dietz wouldn't screw with me."

"Maybe not. But I think Grint and his uncle sure as hell would."

Tate's eyes swept the woods. "Ain't nobody in there."

But something was.

Just the slightest movement. A deer, perhaps. Perhaps not.

High above us dark masses of clouds jostled one another. A humid breeze rose from the swamp, fluttering the leaves and carrying with it the odor of decaying meat. Tate edged a step closer to the forest.

And that much closer to me.

I shoveled the first spade of dirt, then another and another, exaggerating the swing of my arms so that the dirt landed ten feet away. With each motion I glanced at Tate, whose focus stayed trained on the pitch-black spaces between the trees.

There came another movement—the skittering, leaping gray form of some large animal. Tate fired three quick rounds into the darkness. An unearthly shriek resounded throughout the forest, confirming the hit. Bleating half-human cries rent the air for a few seconds, but having leaped into action by then, I hardly noticed them.

Instead of wildly swinging the shovel during the lunge forward, I held it as if it were a lance. That saved a half second; enough to drive the spade under Tate's chin before he could react. While he staggered backward gasping for breath and spurting blood, I smashed his gun hand with my fist. The weapon dropped and he stumbled over a log. I was on top of him like a crab on a snail.

Marine Corps hand-to-hand combat training is something you never forget, but not for the reasons one who has never undergone it would expect. The first thing it emphasizes is that warriorship and sport fighting like boxing and karate are different things. Killing the enemy is the goal of a Marine—and the techniques taught are brutally efficient—but only when it is necessary to preserve one's life or those of innocent others. Combat trainers emphasize the Life Value mechanism so you don't lose sight of your moral compass. The rationale behind it is a practical one: It makes it easier to live with yourself later when the Corps may call upon you to do the same thing again.

Knowing this, it took me about half a second to justify what happened next.

I gouged his eyes with the fingers of my left hand, followed by repeated jabs to his throat with those of my right, and finished by striking my flat right palm into his face until the irises disappeared into his skull.

I hadn't the time or inclination to spend one of the few bullets left in the chamber. Grabbing the car keys from his pocket, I picked up the Magnum and ran to the car, leaving Stormin' Norman Tate to bleed out.

Then I drove like Dale Earnhardt on uppers for Adam's sacrificial altar, desperately hoping I wasn't too late.

Chapter 31

The dirt road forked after a mile. Rather than take a direct route to the altar, I slowed to a near crawl, shut off the headlights, and turned onto a branch leading to a small rise several hundred yards to the west of Tower Hill. It soon became impassable for the Chevrolet. I got out and began walking quickly down a narrow path roughly parallel to where I thought the sacrificial stone would be at the base of the hill.

Thorn trees joined in a spiky arch above my head; sharp nettles cut into my legs as I stumbled and slid down the steep slope. Most of the trees were dead, their gray trunks testament to some disease or destructive beetle. Logs and branches felled by wind or rot lay everywhere on the ground. Even some of the living trees had diseased limbs. It was not a place for living things except, perhaps, for night scavengers.

Forty meters later, panting and sweating, I came to a flat ledge overlooking a precarious cliff, the top of which extended outward ten feet. There was no time to head back up to search for another route.

I stuffed the six-inch barrel of the Magnum in the small of my back and crawled over the side of the breast of rough granite. Almost immediately I found myself in an awkward position, with my legs dangling over empty space. My shoulders and arms carried all my weight as I began to haul myself down by clinging to outcroppings of rock and the more secure roots, scrabbling for a hold wherever I could find it.

Another fifteen feet of this and it was all too clear gravity was winning. To fall meant broken limbs, if not death. I spotted a moss-covered ledge a few feet below and to the left of my position. With willpower born of desperation, I gathered what little strength remained in my arms and hurled myself onto it. It was only about twenty inches wide, but the stone face went inboard a few inches and I was able to land on it with both feet. For a few desperate seconds I tottered on the slippery shelf, until I gained a semblance of control. Nauseous from the exertion, and with chin, chest, and thighs leaning tenuously against the wall, I caught my breath and rested my shaking arms. When I dared to look down, all I could see were the dark outlines of unforgiving boulders and spear-pointed saplings far below.

What a stupid way to die, I thought. With all my mountain-climbing experience, it was beginning to look like I would perish while trying to descend a hill on a warm night in Missouri. Not exactly Mallory-esque.

While struggling to find a hold, I'd been able to rein in fear and even use its testosterone-induced chemicals to power my muscles beyond their normal limits. But now that I was marooned on this mossy rim of rock, unable to move up or down, my energy drained to the point where I couldn't have acted even if a ladder miraculously appeared.

It was a cramp that saved me. I felt it building in my left calf, its pain fierce, as if the muscle in my lower leg were tying itself in a knot. I rose up and down on my toes to try to make it stop, but it only spread the torture to the other limb. My entire body began to spasm uncontrollably, disturbing the swallows nesting in the nooks of the cliff.

Many birds disappeared over the top, but a few, intent on protecting their hatchlings, swarmed around me, diving at my head, squawking their complaints, and beating their wings. To prevent several of the more insistent ones from pecking my eyes, I swiped my arm at them. But the windmill action only disturbed them more, and they continued their relentless attack. A beak struck my neck. Another pecked my cheek. Then another. More birds returned to take part in what had become a frenzied defense of their rooks. Blood streamed down my forehead and cheeks and into my mouth. I continued to swing frantically at the feathered beasts even as I found myself falling.

My hands clutched for the rock I had just stood upon. The jolt nearly jerked my arms out of their sockets. I clung with bleeding hands but began to slide even as my fingernails clawed for whatever resistance could be gained. With my face getting sandpapered by the rough rock, I scratched for anything to slow my descent—hands, toes, elbows, knees—but the momentum couldn't be stopped. A tenth of a second later, I was hurtling down the slope barely in contact with the surface. Any sense of self-preservation deserted me as I prepared for the agony of compound fractures or impalement.

Then, miraculously, I felt a slight outward inclination of the surface. Slight, but certain. Thirty feet later, one of my feet struck the base of a tree that sent me spinning sideways onto a boulder. I tumbled over it, spinning, arms and legs flailing, but slowing, always slowing until coming to a stop in a pile of acorns and deer droppings.

I didn't move for a few seconds in order to take physical inventory. Both knees were sore, my hands were numb, and I was bleeding from head to toe from the scouring I'd got from the rock surface, but nothing seemed broken. I got to my feet a little uncertainly, but not trembling. I took a step. The left knee buckled but held. I'd played rugby with worse.

Hobbling through a grove of pin oaks while ducking to avoid the lower branches I came to a clearing. The thick clouds that obscured the moon made it difficult to survey more than fifty yards, but I could see the shadowy outline of Tower Hill above. The road meandered fifteen meters to my right. I had to be near. Dropping on my belly, I crawled over rough terrain until coming to the trail Josie and I had walked down when we first came upon the altar stone; it felt like an eternity ago. A light flickered in the near distance, but trees and foliage blocked my view. I crept further on my hands and knees, pausing behind a slender tree upon hearing faint voices. My head was still ringing from all the blows it had suffered that day, but there was no mistaking the sound of Lamar's growling truculence and Porter Grint's whine.

I lurched forward a few more yards until coming to

a large round boulder. Getting to my feet, I peered through the leafy branches of the tree in front of it.

The thick oval stone lay twenty-five yards ahead. The squat wooden chair from the house had been placed in its center between a pair of tall wax candles, their flames flickering in the breeze. Beyond the ominous scene was Jacob, his setup work completed, leaning against a pickup on the side of the road.

I could still hear voices but saw no one around the altar. I had the horrible thought that they might be cleaning up after having fulfilled their loathsome oath. Whether or not that was the case, I wasn't about to let them get away with their crime.

I was pondering how when I noticed movement near the road. Porter Grint, bedecked in his temple robe, and Seth haul what looked like a squirming white bag they had pulled from the pickup. As they came closer, I realized it was Natalie, alive and literally kicking. Bless her feisty Irish heart.

Dennis Dietz and Lamar Stagg, also wearing robes, walked a few paces behind, making a grim procession toward the altar of sacrifice.

Only three rounds remained in the cylinder of Tate's revolver. I had qualified "expert" with handguns every year in the Marine Corps, but that was years ago and always on a firing range during daylight hours. While twenty-five yards was a relatively easy range, even for a headshot in poor light, the tremendous noise and muzzle flash would have the secondary targets instantly dropping for cover. I'd likely kill the first person wielding the knife at Natalie's throat—probably Dietz—but the odds were nil that I'd have a second chance before Grint and the others regrouped to get me.

But what choice did I have? Even if Josie had succeeded in contacting Buford Higgins or the police, reinforcements wouldn't arrive in time.

The two men forced Natalie onto the chair and bound her body to it with wide strips of white cloth. In the weak candlelight her face appeared ghostly pale, but far from defeated. Either out of a warped sense of propriety or some twisted protocol requiring that the sacrifice be lucid, she didn't appear to have been drugged.

Having performed his task, Seth stepped from the stone. Lamar and Dietz, each with some difficulty because of their disabilities, joined Grint atop the altar. Standing behind Natalie, Dietz tied a white scarf around her eyes while his uncle and cousin stood beside the respective candles. Then he nodded to indicate all was ready.

Lamar's sudden paroxysm of coughing shattered the night stillness. He bent over in real distress and I began to hope his helpless hacking would postpone the ceremony. But all too soon the geezer straightened up and his spasms ended in a brief series of hiccups. Clearing his throat, he proceeded to pronounce in a raspy rattle:

"Repent ye! Repent, woman; and by your sacrifice wash away the perfidious sin of your ancestor, Thomas Ford. Accept your salvation with fear and trembling before the Lord and be rewarded with everlasting life."

Dietz followed with his practiced lines. "Fear not, Natalie Delaney Phelan, for the Kingdom of God is close at hand. Prepare ye the way of the Lord."

Then it was Grint's turn. He unfolded a piece of notebook paper, held it in the light of a candle, and struggled to read what had been written for him.

"'Know ye the dead shall receive reward after paying pen...penit...penitence for their transmissions.'"

"Transgressions," Dennis Dietz corrected. Then he withdrew from within his robe the bone-handled knife I'd seen at the farmhouse.

I stepped from the boulder for a clearer sight line and assumed a firing position: knees slightly bent, one foot behind the other, upper body squared to the target. Mindful of the Magnum's strong recoil, I gripped the handle of the revolver firmly in both hands keeping thumbs and fingers below the cylinder gap to avoid the escaping compressed gas. I leaned forward, held my arms straight out, and used my dominant eye to line the barrel at a spot one inch above Dennis Dietz's right ear. I pulled back the hammer and placed the tip of my right index finger on the trigger.

Dietz bent over. He clutched the back of Natalie's chignon with his titanium hand and drew back her head.

I adjusted my aim and squeezed the trigger.

Click.

Misfire. Rare for a revolver.

I stroked the trigger again.

Click.

With my thumb I felt the firing pin that was attached to the hammer. It felt jagged instead of smooth.

Broken. Useless.

The knife in Dietz's good hand hovered next to Natalie's throat. There was a rustling of the leaves as the wind picked up, extinguishing one of the candles.

Then everything froze.

At first I thought the sound came from the throat

of a very large cat—rare sightings of cougars had been reported in northwest Missouri for years. But what followed was something far different. How to describe it?

Think of the mournful yowl of a starving child, the tortured screech of a hare caught in a trap; a thousand other harrowing images increased in vehemence with each passing minute until reaching a spectral intensity so loud and long as to be beyond an earthly source. When it finally ended, it did so in a protracted wail full of such agony and despair as to make Charles Manson weep.

With the last note, the clouds parted. The liberated full moon shone its beams upon the gauzy image of a shimmering figure dressed in a loose-flowing, fantastic garment. Crowned with a tangled mass of silvery hair, the gray skin tightly drawn over facial bones like a mummy, it looked ages old, as if it had been buried and dug up again.

"Elohim! Jehovah! Adam!" Seth screamed from the foot of the altar while pointing to the summit of Tower Hill. "Sweet heavens, what can it be?"

Damned if I knew. But Denny Dietz had a pretty good idea.

His titanium hand released its grip on Natalie Phelan's head.

Chapter 32

The moon retreated behind the clouds and the figure dissolved in darkness.

Dropping the blade onto the rock, Dietz declared, "Enough! As God tested Abraham with Isaac, so he has tested us and shown his mercy for the lamb. Our oath is fulfilled."

"That was no archangel," Lamar snarled between choking gasps, "only that witch of a girl." His face was a cadaverous yellow in the glow of the candle.

Looking back on it, I can't say whether Denny Dietz truly believed what we saw was a guardian spirit. I do know, however, how I was affected by the other-worldly sounds and sight of that moon-christened being on the hill. To this day, I'm not entirely convinced it was Claire.

"The atonement is honored," Dietz insisted. "God has spoken through his holy messenger."

While these words were being said, Grint recovered the knife.

"Blasphemy!" the old man sputtered. He turned to

Seth and Jacob. "Quickly, get after her. Don't fail this time."

While the two began their sprint up the hill, Lamar turned to Grint and very deliberately commanded, "You…will finish…God's work."

Grint hesitated. "The girl, Uncle…"

"Yes, yes, son. She is yours once they catch her. Get on with your duty."

By then, I'd begun my dash to the altar, but it was Dietz who tackled his knife-wielding cousin. They fell in a heap at Natalie's feet, scratching and tearing at each other in deadly earnest. Lamar hollered at them to stop, but Grint's arm jerked outward then back, driving the blade deep into his cousin's armpit.

Dietz groaned as blood spurted from his chest, painting both of their robes muddy red. Despite his death agonies, the former marine's bionic hand made a frantic grab for Grint's wrist and held it, allowing the human one to wrench the bone handle away. With superhuman effort, he fended off his cousin's desperate jabs to plunge the point deep into Grint's neck. A ghastly wail was followed by a convulsive twist, then both fell silent.

At least that's how I pictured it happening. I'd heard the grunts and agonized cries, but didn't see much of the action because I was occupied at the time with Uncle Lamar. For an octogenarian with a bad hip and diseased lungs, he was a gnarly dude who could counterpunch with hands still hard as whalebone. And he fought dirty—after I'd finally cold-cocked him with the butt of the revolver, I had to pull his dentures out of my forearm.

Blood covered every inch of the altar—the scene made even more garish in the flickering light of the remaining candle—and as I watched volumes of it oozing off the flat stone, I couldn't help but think that the vow of Alonzo Stagg had been fulfilled after all.

Lamar, unconscious, had begun to hemorrhage from the lungs. There was no sound, no coughing as rivulets of blood seeped through his lips onto his chin and chest. He was clearly dying and no longer a threat. I turned my attention to Natalie.

"You're safe," I said, removing the cloth that had covered her eyes and mouth. She didn't hear me, for she had passed out.

Leaving her secured in the chair, I moved to where Grint's corpse lay atop his cousin and shoved him to the side. Denny's face, pale as bleached wood, was no longer handsome. The eye patch had come off during the brief fight and the cavity was filled with blood. His jaw hung unnaturally slack so that his mouth was wide open. He might have swallowed his tongue. I didn't bother searching for a pulse. I had started to turn away when suddenly his lips quivered and the lone eye shot open to study me with a long, empty stare. It was a simple muscle retraction that had nothing to do with life, but it startled the hell out of me.

I wanted to say something like, "You did the decent thing, Marine." But it seemed awfully trite and there was no time for sentiment or even ministering to Natalie, not with the two armed Danites chasing after Claire.

Withdrawing the sacrificial knife from Grint's neck, I bolted up Tower Hill, leaving Denny's dead eye gazing at eternity.

A hundred strides later, the hoot of an owl stopped me.

"Claire?" I called softly. "Where are you?"

No answer. Again I ran, my eyes sweeping the dark, crashing headlong through thornbushes, adding my own blood to that from the two corpses that covered me.

Suddenly, I felt as much as heard the swoosh of wings over my head. The owl had settled on the middle branch of a ragged pine. I slowed to a walk. At the base of the tree was a faint spot of light. Moving closer, I saw the prostrate body of Claire Phelan, still dressed in her school uniform. Around her head and shoulders was the white T-shirt that had been used to gag her.

Anxiously, I knelt beside her and whispered her name. She didn't respond.

I touched her forehead and brushed back her silvery hair. Her chest rose and fell in soft breaths. The skin on her neck felt warm and there was an even pulse. She seemed to be in a deep sleep. There were no signs of injury. Gently I picked her up and carried her down to the dirt road, where I placed her in the backseat of Tate's Chevrolet. Then I returned for Natalie.

She was awake now and strangely calm. Cutting her bindings with the knife, I told her Claire was safe, but that Seth and Jacob were still out there armed with rifles. I offered to carry her, but she said she could walk. Moments later, she was in the back seat of the Chevrolet, cradling her daughter in her arms. I started the engine and drove away from the scene of slaughter without turning on the lights.

We were a half mile or so from reaching the parking lot entrance of Adam-ondi-Ahman when a shot rang out and the back window exploded. Anguished cries engulfed the Chevy as the shattered glass spattered over Natalie and Claire. I pounded the steering wheel while uttering a string of obscenities and floored the accelerator. The car leaped forward, and I thought for a moment we were out of range, but a second burst soon destroyed a front tire.

The tortured sound of flayed rubber slapping against the side panels accompanied the car's violent swerve to the left while I struggled with every sinew to maintain control. But there was no stopping two tons of skidding steel going sixty miles per hour on a loose gravel road. The car smashed through a rail fence, hurtled over an embankment and rolled twice before landing on the driver's side in a splintering crash of metal and glass.

Radiator steam poured from the hood. The pungent odor of gasoline filled the interior. Blood trickled from an ear as I fought to clear my head. A heavy groan from behind brought me to my senses. I slid from behind the steering wheel and shifted my body to peer into the back.

Natalie, her right forearm dangling unnaturally, lay crumpled against her daughter.

"Can either of you hear me?" I asked softly. "We must get out. Now."

Natalie's body stiffened. She moaned, "How…Claire?"

A few heartbeats later, we heard a stoic voice whisper, "I'm okay. I…I think."

"Good girl," I said while stretching up to reach the rear door handle. "You'll have to help me get your mother out."

The latch clicked, but the door didn't budge.

The growing pool of gasoline at my feet provided all the motivation I needed to try again. Bursting with adrenaline, I braced my feet against the floorboards and shot upwards, ramming my shoulder against the door panel directly under the lock.

I heard something crack. Instead of my collarbone being broken—given the pain resulting from my effort, that was my first thought—the noise was of metal or plastic jolted loose within the door. A slight tremor reverberated throughout the framework of the car. Then, as I reached again for the door handle, a sudden shift of balance made the effort unnecessary.

The effect of my weight slamming into the door had tipped the Chevy so that it landed right-side-up. The resulting impact opened the door, and after climbing out, I gently reached under Natalie's shoulders. Ignoring her desperate groans and with Claire helping from behind, we eased her from the car. I held her upright as she struggled to stand by herself. The bottom half of her dress was soaked with gasoline.

I looked into her tense, white face. Her eyes were fathomless at first, but soon the blankness left, and she held my gaze.

"Buck up, woman," I hissed. "Your arm is broken, not your legs. We've got to move."

Natalie, her mouth clamped shut, took a tentative step, then another, and we scrambled into a field of sunflowers before she collapsed in agony.

Although it seemed like an eternity, less than a couple of minutes had elapsed since the crash, and while free of the fire danger, we hadn't made it to the cover of trees. To confirm our perilous situation, a new round of bullets zipped through the yellow petals near my head.

"Run, Claire," I urged as we ducked among the sunflowers.

"Not this time."

"You must," I said.

Another round buzzed over our heads like mad hornets. It only made her more adamant.

"I'm not leaving her this time."

I nodded in resignation. There would be no more miracles. The girl lay protectively by her mother while I crouched in front of them, knife in hand, and waited for the avenging angels.

Some say hope is only a gentler name for fear, but I'll take it anytime over despair. When times are at their rawest, I've always been willing to grasp at any shadow, especially now when I heard sirens wailing in the distance.

I saw the rotating sapphire and red lights of the highway patrol cars a few minutes later. They were a quarter of a mile away, speeding in the direction of the altar. I dashed for the road just as the first cruiser barreled over the rise. I leaped into the road desperately waving my hands. Three more cruisers sped past without slowing, but the fourth slid to a stop in front of me.

Squinting over the glare of the headlights, I saw Trooper Buzard behind the wheel.

And Josie Majansik riding shotgun.

Chapter 33

I f the axiom is true that marriages are best made of dissimilar material, the union of Emery and Natalie promised to be everlasting. Still, Josie tells me I shouldn't have said it at their reception. I reminded her that wit is an essential element when giving the Best Man speech.

"There's a thin line between wit and insolence," my beloved said.

"It got a laugh."

"A laugh. One. From Natalie, not Emery."

"I rest my case."

"Oh, Bevan. You may have grown tall, but you've yet to grow up."

I took that as a compliment.

It seemed like everyone in the Irish community had nothing better to do that August afternoon than come down to the Celtic Center to watch a Jack Mormon exchange vows with a lapsed Catholic. Kansas City paddies weren't the only ones in attendance, however.

There was the usual contingent of Riverrun Irregulars and a scrum's worth of ruggers, the latter enticed by rumors of free food, booze, and sprightly Irish dancers. Joe Tuitama arrived with a basket of fruit and fifteen flower-bedecked relatives who promptly settled in a circle and chattered among themselves in Samoan. Opposite them in a far corner of the library under a Celtic cross, Buford Higgins and Trooper Buzard yukked it up over God knows what—probably the nine hundred dollar traffic ticket I had yet to pay, pending appeal. It seems Buford had once taken Lenny Buzard upon his wing when the trooper was just a sixteen-year-old hell-raiser who'd spent time in juvenile detention. Good thing, too, since it was Buford who confirmed Josie's bona fides to Buzard when she flagged down the latter's patrol car for help.

Emery's parents had returned to Utah, but not before giving the couple a new convertible as a wedding present.

Not surprisingly, Emery's other relatives were conspicuously absent. Uncle Lamar had died from loss of blood soon after being scooped off the altar at Adam-ondi-Ahman. As for the Danite boys, Seth and Jacob sat in the Daviess County jail awaiting trial for kidnapping, murder, child endangerment, and a dozen other counts. They were represented by a public defender, no one in their extended families wishing or able to pay for their defense.

It's not as if they were missed for the wedding.

At one o'clock, a bell was rung and the crowd took their seats. Sandra Epstein played "Red is the Rose" on her flute as Natalie and Emery walked hand in hand to the front of the room.

On the one day when most women indulge in excessive dress—jewelry, makeup, and fancy lace—

Natalie had chosen the opposite. With her arm encased in a fiberglass cast, it would have looked ridiculous to parade in a traditional flowing gown. But I think she would have chosen this understated look no matter what. It fit the change in her.

The only adornments she wore were tiny, imperfect natural pearl earrings. Her pale blue dress with its subtle V-neck and delicate cap sleeves fit her tall, lissome figure beautifully—Barbara Scanlon, a seamstress in Parkville, had personally seen to that. Natalie's auburn hair lay curtained over her shoulder in a gentle braid. Her skin was radiant and fresh, the freckles across the bridge of her nose adding a charming definition to her rosy complexion. There was no flamboyant nail polish today; just simple, open hands reaching out to Emery.

As stunning as her outfit was, the feature most striking was her expression of complete and utter joy.

The ceremony conducted by a Unitarian minister was as touching and dignified as it was brief. In contrast to the radiant beauty standing beside him, however, Emery looked like death warmed over. It wasn't because of his injuries—he was close to a full recovery—but from the sheer horror of being the center of attention in front of two hundred people.

When I mentioned this to Josie, she whispered, "On the contrary, I find such diffidence extremely attractive in a man, particularly one so bright. I also suspect a sexual dynamo lurks beneath that shy facade."

She followed that with a dart aimed at my ego— something about "envy being another form of praise." Then, as if to prove her point, when the I dos were exchanged and the pronouncing done, Emery swept his bride into his arms and planted a kiss on her that made even me blush.

Some people have no sense of shame.

While Josie and I stood in line for wedding cake, a ruddy-faced man with a chest like a pouter pigeon and enormous hands introduced himself to us. His name was Ezekiel Larsen, the caretaker at Adam-ondi-Ahman, whom Emery had made a special point to invite.

"It grieved me to learn of the trouble you experienced on our grounds," Larsen said, with only the slightest emphasis on the 'our.' He reached into his pocket and handed me his business card. "Please consider a return visit under more favorable circumstances. We try our best to maintain a tranquil atmosphere of peace and quiet reflection."

Voices don't always match faces, but Larsen's did. Both were warm and inviting.

After thanking him and apologizing for whatever part we played in bringing notoriety to such a sacred place, he assured us the Church was grateful that we had thwarted an unspeakable crime.

"By the way," Josie added, "we were impressed with the young missionary we met when we first arrived at the property. She was obviously dedicated to her job and very helpful to us."

Larsen looked perplexed. "She? You mean the lad, don't you? Willy Tanner, from Utah?"

"Oh, no," responded Josie. "It was a young woman, absolutely. She had lovely blond hair tied back with a red cloth and was picking up litter along the gravel road. I distinctly remember her long blue skirt, which struck me as a little odd for such a hot day; but she looked very official, if not somewhat distant."

I chimed in, "It was getting dark and she cautioned that the gates would soon close. But when I asked where we could find Tower Hill she seemed to take on a different persona and didn't hesitate to give directions. She even advised there would be a full moon that night."

The caretaker's eyes narrowed.

"I'm afraid I have no idea what you're talking about. We've had no women on mission this year; only Willy and another young man who didn't start until this month."

The color rose in his cheeks. "Furthermore," he said, his voice rising, "I'm certain that Willy Tanner would never have brought a female guest to the property during his mission service. We have very strict rules about that. It wouldn't be appropriate."

Josie and I exchanged looks. There was no point in trying to convince him.

Starting to reach for a slice of cake to give to him, Josie asked, "Chocolate or vanilla?"

"Neither, thank you," he replied, patting his ample stomach. "Now, if you folks will excuse me, I'm off to congratulate the newlyweds."

Josie picked up a piece of vanilla after he'd gone.

"What just happened here?" she asked. "I remember that girl as if I saw her yesterday."

"Beats me," I said. "All I know is that we could use a drink."

"You go ahead," Josie told me. "The last thing I want is for my mind to get any fuzzier."

Wandering to the bar, I saw Renata Wormington, the curator at the Spencer Library. It was the first time I'd seen her since we'd met at the scene of the fire in Lawrence.

She thanked me for helping recover at least some of the books Mr. Tate stole from Eulalia Darp, adding, "God only knows what he sold over the years."

"I was just trying to stay alive. What did you find at his place?"

"Some interesting books were packed in his tiny apartment, but few were particularly outstanding. Most involved Native American history. The values ranged from five hundred to a thousand dollars, with a few notable exceptions. There was a very nice two-volume, third edition of Manners, Customs and Condition of the North American Indians by George Catlin, for example, and a nice association copy of The Vanishing American by Zane Grey, which the author had inscribed to his niece. Tate even kept a Chippewa Bible. I wonder how things might have been different if Eula had shown him more appreciation."

Remembering how the evil brute had ordered me to dig my own grave, I thought Ms. Wormington was being a tad generous. But it didn't seem the right moment to suggest Stormin' Norman was the last person to deserve a helping hand.

"I'm glad what survived will go to the Spencer," I said instead.

"Yes, we should be grateful for that," she sighed. "But it tears me apart thinking of how much was lost in the fire."

After the barkeep had poured our two pints, Renata suggested that I join her in a corner.

"I heard you recovered the inscribed Book of Mormon. Congratulations."

"Thanks. I was certain it had been lost in the blaze."

"What does Emery Stagg intend to do with it

now?"

"He's agreed to sell it to the Harold Lee Library at BYU for two hundred thousand dollars. He feels it's the least he can do for the trouble his family has caused."

"He's not exactly giving it away."

"Yes and no. He and Natalie are keeping ninety percent, but giving twenty thousand to the Celtic Heritage Center."

"What about your commission?"

I smiled. "Renata, after all that's happened, that's the last thing I care about having. Call it my wedding gift to Natalie and Emery."

"Well, maybe I can add a little more sunlight to your day."

I held her pint while she fussed around in her purse, finally pulling out an envelope.

"What's that?"

"The copy of a letter I sent along with Eulalia's endorsement for your admittance to the ABAA."

"Eulalia's endorsement?"

"Yes. The dear old thing gave it to me—while asking me to endorse you as well—the day before she died. You know how meticulous about those things she was. You'll be getting official notification from the Board next week."

And that kind of news had me floating on a cloud into the main room where Aidan Delahunt was serenading the newlyweds with a beautiful rendition of Van Morrison's "Irish Heartbeat."

I found Josie, held her by the waist and together we mouthed the words sung by the troubadour:

"Oh, won't you stay,

Stay a while with your own ones

'Cause the world is so cold…"

The song ended with champagne and all manner of toasts and congratulations, but before people began filing out, Emery walked onto the low stage—the very one upon which Liam O'Halloran had danced his last.

For a moment, he appeared discombobulated. His head dipped and his thoughts seemed to desert him. After gazing at the throng for an interminable minute, however, he summoned Natalie and Claire to his side. Clearing his throat, he thanked everyone for coming and proceeded to say what was in his heart to the hushed crowd.

"Getting what you most desire is never easy. You constantly explore options that you think you need to obtain happiness—a good career, a fine house, a belief in something. But what we truly want visits us only in our dreams…"

Emery seemed to draw life from his words. After pausing to catch his breath, he resumed in a voice that had deepened and grown stronger.

"I always yearned for a family to call my own. For one reason or another, however, it eluded me. Fulfillment, I thought, must lie elsewhere. Years passed and the dream was replaced by a far less noble obsession. I'd forgotten it, but the dream did not forget me."

Then, spreading his arms around his new wife and stepdaughter, Emery bestowed a blessing upon them that managed to clog the tear ducts of even the ruggers in the audience.

"Natalie, Claire, a chuisle, a chroí, is tu mo ghra." Irish for "my pulse, my heart, I love you."

"What did I tell ya?" Josie said, her voice quavering as we headed from the Center to our car. "Natalie's the lucky one."

Chapter 34

September arrived and the Aspen Ruggerfest loomed—not to mention our own upcoming nuptials.

All things considered, life was looking rosier than a Laplander's bottom. Not only had everyone I cared about survived, but Emery Stagg's rare Mormon book had been recovered, along with my reputation. I was about to become a member of the Antiquarian Book Association of America with all the honors and privileges that entailed, and I wasn't required to sell a fourth of Riverrun's inventory overnight just to stay afloat.

And lest one forget the complication involving my familial relations, even that seemed to have worked itself out.

Surprised as Alice Winter was to discover that my daughter Annie batted for the other team—Alice's phrase, not mine—she was thrilled that the kids could remain close and still keep Mark's paternity a secret. It didn't matter that maintaining that last fantasy was like putting retreads on tires sure to come off five thousand highway miles later; it satisfied everyone for the time being.

"Yes, life is good," I muttered in our upstairs bedroom as I packed cleats, mouth guard, surgical tape, Icy Hot gel, shorts, and Vaseline into my rugby kit bag.

Josie looked up from her suitcase that held an assortment of nylon stockings, lacy silk undergarments, and a bridal garter.

"What'd you say, darling?"

"I was thinking how lucky we are."

"We sure are." She stuffed a pair of hiking boots next to her high-heeled shoes, then asked, "Did you confirm the time with the minister?"

"Not to worry, my love. Reverend Alexander has promised to officiate right after our first match."

"But he's a tight head prop. Oh, sweetie, promise me he won't be all bloody."

"We'll hose off together. I promise."

"Gee, thanks."

After checking the tickets for when our flight was to depart for Aspen, she curled up on the bed.

"Michael?"

"Yes?"

"I got you a wedding present."

"Ahh, babe! I thought we agreed to wait until after the wedding to exchange gifts."

"I know, but I couldn't wait to surprise you. Anyway, this one's mostly for Riverrun."

"Okay. What is it?"

"I'll tell you, but first, is there anything you're keeping from me?"

That sure came out of left field. Planting an

angelic smile on my face, I searched my memory bank for any major transgressions that I'd failed to mention. Naturally, I came up empty.

"I told you about fathering Mark as soon as I learned of it," I finally answered. "And while I tend to cheat on crossword puzzles, I certainly never considered murdering you. So, no, I don't have any…" I caught myself before I said skeletons in my closet. "Why do you ask?"

"It sure would be nice not to be surprised after our marriage."

"Couldn't agree more," I said, relaxing. "Now, what did you get me?"

"You know how you're always complaining about not having enough table space in the shop's basement storeroom?"

"Yeah?"

"Well, I found a great workstation at IKEA, and knowing how you hate to assemble things, I hired their people to install it. They'll even take away the old file cabinet—"

"Huh?" I gasped. "When are they coming?"

"Tomorrow, after we've gone to Aspen. I left word with Deirdre Lescalle to let them in."

"But…but what about all the important stuff that's in the cabinet?"

"There was only a 2010 sales ledger, three years of canceled checks, the box of staples…"

My mind whirled. "You mean you've been in it?"

"I'm afraid so." She wrinkled her nose and held up the key to the file cabinet. "You see, I've been a bit of a sneak, too. That was my little secret I wanted to share."

We grabbed a bottle of Irish whiskey from the

kitchen and drove straight to Riverrun and the store-room. Before opening the filing cabinet, I turned to Josie.

"Cripes, what you must think of me. Do you think I'm crazy?"

"A little," she said, kissing my forehead. "But what happened to you in New Zealand was enough to upset anyone's sense of equilibrium. I only wish you'd thought that I was all you needed to get right again."

"I know that now. Please believe me."

"Of course I do. Now formally introduce me to the Captain, so we can be done with it."

I opened the filing cabinet, removed the bag, and placed it on the table.

"If it's okay with you," Josie pleaded, "don't uncover him. Seeing him once was enough for me."

I had no problem with that. Captain Cook's remains, like Hungarian wine, had not traveled well.

"Well then," I said, pouring the whiskey into two coffee cups. "Here's a toast to an old friend tried and true. Sláinte!"

We gulped our drinks and then I wrapped the skull in cellophane bubble wrap and sealed it in a box cushioned with Styrofoam. After inserting a typed note explaining as much as the circumstances warranted without identifying us, I addressed it to Solomon Pualinui, a modern descendant of King Kalani'opu'u in the town of Kealakekua Bay, Kona Coast, Hawaii.

He would know to return it to the cliffs above the Captain's beloved sea.